Beauty and the Baron

by Joanna Barker

Titles by Joanna Barker

The Truth about Miss Ashbourne
Beauty and the Baron
Miss Adeline's Match (Coming April 2019)

Beauty AND THE BARON

JOANNA BARKER

Cover design: Blue Water Books

Joanna Barker
https://www.authorjoannabarker.com

First Printing: January 2019

To anyone who has ever loved the magic

and romance of fairy tales.

“Perhaps the dreadful fate which appears

to await me conceals another

as happy as this seems terrible.”

—Madame de Villeneuve

(*La Belle et la Bête*, trans. by J. R. Planché)

Chapter One

Rose Sinclair prided herself on being an excellent walker. She could wander for hours on end throughout the countryside without tiring, with only the wind and clouds as her companions.

But now, stopping beside the brick pillars that marked the drive leading to Norcliffe House, she found it necessary to pause and catch her breath. Not from exhaustion, but from the intimidating sight that met her eyes. The manor loomed in the distance, soaring Grecian columns guarding the wide front steps, enormous diamond-paned windows dark against the aged brick of its walls. The center portion of the house towered above the wings that branched out on either side.

Rose swallowed, her eyes following the sharp lines of the building, tracing the immaculately groomed gardens and lawns to the edge of the wooded hills. Was she truly going to do this? Begging an audience with Lord Norcliffe was likely the worst idea she had ever had, even above cutting her hair to her ears at the age of fourteen. The baron had earned himself quite the reputation, and if the rumors were to be believed, he was as rude as he was rich. Based on the opulence of his estate, he must be boorish indeed.

But her options were few and her coins even fewer. She tightened the ribbons of her bonnet and pressed forward, determined not to let her fears catch hold of her.

Rose arrived at the low steps and marched up, trying to ignore the elaborate stone carvings surrounding the columns and the daunting height of the door. She allowed herself one quick, deep breath before she struck the knocker against the door. Footsteps sounded from inside and the door opened, soundless on well-oiled hinges. A footman stood there, dressed in fine livery, and looking none too pleased to see her.

"If you're here about the maid position," he said with a frown, "you ought to know better than to come to the front door."

He made to close the door and Rose—in her shock—nearly let him. But she came to herself in time, placing a hand on the door before it could close.

"No," she managed. "I'm not here about the post. I've come to see Lord Norcliffe."

The footman eyed her in disbelief. "You have an appointment with the baron?"

"Yes." Rose attempted to keep her eyes wide and innocent. Lying did not come easily to her on the best of days, and this was clearly not the best of days. "If you would be so kind as to inform him that Miss Rose Sinclair is here, I would be most appreciative."

The footman sighed and allowed her inside. Rose fought back her own sigh of relief. Her task was far from over.

"Wait here." The footman turned and walked down an airy, carpeted hallway, lined with gilded artwork and statues balancing on tiny tables. It was eerily quiet, her ears accustomed to bustling village life. Even the smell was different here, musty and deep compared to the fresh summer air of her walk.

She watched as the footman entered a dark-stained wooden door. She could only imagine the conversation taking place inside. She had never before met Lord Norcliffe, and even if the footman believed her, the baron would know for a fact that she had not requested an audience with him. But Papa was depending on her. She had to try, even if she failed horribly in the attempt.

When the footman opened the door once again, she looked up at him, half expecting a scowl and an instant dismissal. But he gestured at the open door. "Lord Norcliffe will see you."

Rose blinked and then nodded as if she had expected such a response. In truth, she had not anticipated making it this far. The swarm of nerves inside her took flight like bees around a hive. But she could not hesitate now. With a swift brush to her skirts and a steadying breath, she strode down the hall and into the room.

The baron sat across the length of the room, behind a massive desk framed by floor-to-ceiling windows. He did not look up at her entrance, his eyes fixed instead on the ledger open before him.

She eyed him as she approached, a bit taken aback. From the rumors that ran rampant in the village, she'd rather expected a more fearsome appearance, a jagged scar or dark, cruel features. As it was, his light hair and slim build were more suited to a London dandy than the most feared and unpleasant nobleman in the county.

He still did not look up, his eyes moving over the page. Rose's feet slowed and she came to an awkward halt in the center of the room. Ought she sit in one of the armchairs before his desk? That did not seem right. How was one supposed to greet a baron exactly? A curtsy, no doubt, but what was she to do if the man refused to look at her? This was the first time she had ever regretted reading under her desk during etiquette classes at boarding school.

Rose did not dare move, her shallow breaths deafening in the quiet room. Finally—finally—the baron looked up, his eyes narrowed on hers as he set aside his ledger. She gulped. He was handsome, with a strong jaw and striking features, far younger than she'd imagined. He could not be much older than her four and twenty years. She dipped into a curtsy, knees trembling beneath her skirts.

"I do not recall setting a meeting for this morning." His voice was a sharp baritone, his eyes such a light blue they appeared nearly grey. "But as you have found your purpose important enough to lie, my curiosity got the better of me."

Rose gripped her reticule, her face flooding with heat. She had practiced this conversation dozens of times in her mind over the past two days, but never had it started like *this*. She avoided the accusation, knowing there was nothing she could say in her defense.

"Lord Norcliffe, my name is Rose Sinclair," she began, her voice weaker than she would have liked. "I have a proposition that I believe will equally benefit both of us."

"A proposition?" he repeated harshly. "What can *you* possibly offer me?"

Rose might have been irritated by the self-importance in his question if she was not so very terrified of him. She clasped her shaking hands behind her back and lifted her chin.

"I know you recently lost your steward," she said. "He took another position in Herefordshire, if the rumors in town are to be believed."

Lord Norcliffe did not seem surprised that his household was a topic of discussion amongst the locals. He merely leaned back in his chair, his eyes still scrutinizing her intensely. Rose took his silence as permission to continue.

"Mr. Turner could not have left you at a worse time," she said. "The harvest is in a few weeks, and—"

"And what, Miss Sinclair?" His eyes were hard, unforgiving. "You are putting yourself forward as his replacement?"

"Not as a replacement, exactly." Only the fact that she had practiced her lines unceasingly allowed her voice any amount of confidence. "I know part of Mr. Turner's responsibilities was keeping the financial records of the estate. I have some experience in this area and wanted to offer my services to you until such time that you find a worthy candidate to act as steward."

He raised his eyebrow with a mocking gleam. "'Some experience?' Do tell."

She cleared her throat. "I've managed the finances for my father's business the last six years, and have done so quite effectively, resulting in balanced books and a turn of profit every year."

"What business is this?"

Rose had known the question was coming, and yet now that it was upon her, she found she could hardly speak.

"Sinclair's Bookshop," she finally forced out.

Lord Norcliffe's already intense eyes darkened. He rose to his feet, balancing on his knuckles as he leaned across the desk with barely concealed anger. "I thought I recognized your name." He spoke in a low, dangerous tone. "You would dare come here and ask for work, when your own father is a scheming thief who owes money to half the town, including myself?"

His accusations pierced her, hurting all the more because of their truth. But it was still her father he was speaking of. "He is not a thief," she said quietly. "He is only guilty of making a terrible decision, for which he is quite remorseful."

He shook his head in disbelief. "Terrible decision? The man gambled away a dozen different loans, without any intent to pay them back. Debtor's prison is no more than he deserves."

Rose closed her eyes. Oh, if only he knew how wrong he was. Papa had been a fool, yes, but he did not deserve to live in such deprivation as existed in Marshalsea. She had visited him once since he had been reported by his creditors, and the memory was a black abyss in her mind—the stench, the filth, the vermin. She opened her eyes again, slowly letting out her breath.

"My lord," she began, "whatever my father may have done, I had no part in it. He kept his debts separate from the bookshop's finances, which were impeccable, I assure you." She did not bother to add that she had been completely ignorant of his debts until it all came crashing down upon them both. "And I wish you to know I have repaid all his loans but one. It was my hope that you would allow me to settle his remaining debt to you by working off the amount."

Lord Norcliffe scowled at her. "You must be mad to think I would allow you anywhere near my books. Even ignoring your unfortunate parentage, running an estate's finances is vastly more complicated than managing a mere shop, and you are far from qualified. Now leave at once before I lose my temper entirely."

He sat back at his desk and pulled his ledger to him. Rose stood frozen, her feet unable to move, her lungs burning with the effort to breathe. This had been her last hope. Her father was in prison, her mother long dead, and no relatives to speak of. No one in town would hire her, for the same reasons as he had tortured her with. She had already sold everything to pay Papa's debts—the books, their furniture, and even the bookshop itself—but it wasn't enough. And still she must pay for his food and rent at Marshalsea. Such was the irony of debtor's prison, that most who entered would never escape because of their prison fees. Starvation was a real and frightening possibility for many. Even Papa.

"Please." Her voice was barely above a whisper. "I beg you to reconsider."

Lord Norcliffe did not look up, but his jaw tightened as he stared unblinking at the page before him.

"My lord," she said, allowing the desperation inside her to color her tone. Because what else could she do? If he turned her away, she had no friends, no family who would take her in. "I have nowhere else to go."

Henry Covington, the Baron Norcliffe, stared at the ledger before him, the words and sums an unreadable mess thanks to the haze of anger in his eyes. What was this woman thinking? Did she truly believe he could employ her after her father's crimes? Mr. Sinclair had come to him months ago, seeking a loan to expand his bookshop. It was a good investment, considering the popularity of the shop. But the money had never been invested. The blasted fool had gambled away the entire loan. There were few people so loathsome as a debtor, and Henry had little forgiveness for the crime.

"Please," came Miss Sinclair's voice again, hoarse and quavering.

He gritted his teeth. *She is only attempting to play upon your heartstrings*. Her father was a liar and thief, and there was no use entertaining any thought that she was different.

Henry looked up, the words already forming on his tongue. But they ceased as he took in her red, tear-filled eyes, her hands clasped before her as if in prayer. If she *was* pretending, then she was a talented actress indeed. Not to mention as stunning a woman as he had ever seen. Arresting brown eyes, delicate features, and a figure that drew his eye too easily.

But he had seen many a pretty face during his time in Society, and hers would not be his undoing now.

"There is not the slightest possibility I would allow you to manage my books," he said flatly.

Miss Sinclair did not move for the longest moment and then she gave a nod, an odd, jerky motion that tore her eyes from his.

"I—I understand." Her voice was faded, as if she had already left the room. "Th—thank you for your time."

She gave a wobbling curtsy and met his eyes once more, her gaze almost wild with distress. Then she turned and walked toward the door, her head bowed and steps heavy.

The sight brought a flash of memory to him, of another woman walking away from him, the last sight he would ever see of her. Even now, the thought of his mother—and his father—brought a sharp ache to his chest. What would Mother have thought of his actions today? He tried to shake off the thought. It did not matter.

But the thought refused to dissipate, instead growing stronger in his mind. Mother would never have turned Miss Sinclair away. *Kindness matters most when it is hardest to give*, she always said.

And would never say again.

"Wait."

The word left Henry's mouth before he even realized he had made a decision. Miss Sinclair came to an abrupt stop. What the devil was he thinking? His mind worked frantically as he stood again, attempting to recapture his focus.

She turned back to look at him, blinking rapidly, clearly trying to hide the onset of tears. Were all women so prone to crying? He could hardly say. Two years of self-imposed solitude had rendered him quite out of touch with the gentler sex.

He glanced down at his desk, littered with letters and books, and his eye caught upon a note from Mrs. Morton. An idea came to him then. "My housekeeper is in need of a maid-of-all-work."

Miss Sinclair stared at him, as if he had just sprouted antlers from his head. "And you are offering the position to me?"

He narrowed his eyes at the disbelief in her voice. Was she offended by his offering such a low job to her? She might have been raised middle-class, but her father's actions had lowered her far beyond that now. "If such a post is not *beneath* you."

She shook her head, as if she had not even noticed his curt tone. "No, of course it is not. But I've no recommendations, and I'm not certain I even have the knowledge—"

"Are you attempting to convince me *not* to hire you?" Henry fixed her with the severe glare that came all too naturally to him these days. "Because you are doing a deucedly good job of it."

She took a long, deep breath, staring at her feet. Then she looked up and met his eyes with a gentle smile. "I am grateful for your offer, and I accept."

Her smile set him at odds. No one smiled at him, least of all a woman who would likely work years in his employ for a debt she had not incurred. He cleared his throat. "This will be, of course, under the same terms as your previous proposition." He sat once again. "All wages will be forfeited until your father's debt to me is repaid."

Miss Sinclair nodded eagerly, eyes bright with hope. But then she bit her lip. "I am sorry to ask this of you, after the generosity of your offer. But I must pay my father's prison fees. Might I take a portion of my earnings and send it to him each month?"

He exhaled in exasperation, wanting nothing more than to refuse her request. But he had already promised her the position, and he never went back on his word.

"Very well." He spoke in a gruff tone, wanting to make clear he was none too pleased with the arrangement. "But if your work is found to be unsatisfactory in any way, do not think I will hesitate to dismiss you."

She pulled her chin back, her eyes wide, and Henry almost regretted the harshness of his words. But it was better to be clear from the start what his expectations were. He would not be taken advantage of again.

"Of course," she said softly. "I understand. I am a hard worker and fast learner. I promise you will not regret your offer."

Henry stifled the urge to groan. She couldn't know that he already regretted it. He'd suffered a moment of weakness and she had certainly gotten the better end of this arrangement.

Blast his sentimentality.

And blast Miss Sinclair's beautiful eyes shining with a gleam of hope.

Chapter Two

"Across the hall you'll find the billiards room, and the library next." Mrs. Morton spoke in a brusque, toneless voice as she marched down the main hallway of Norcliffe House. Rose had to take two steps for every one of the housekeeper's long, purposeful strides. In the fastest quarter hour of Rose's life, they'd already seen all the rooms belowstairs—the kitchen, servants' hall, scullery, and more—and they had moved on to the upper floors.

"Lord Norcliffe's study." Mrs. Morton nodded at another door up ahead. Rose barely had the chance to recognize it from the previous day before the housekeeper continued speaking with a frown. "Which you already know."

Rose gulped. Clearly Mrs. Morton did not appreciate having an inexperienced maid forced upon her. It would be an uphill battle to win her good opinion.

Rose eyed the study door as they passed. Was Lord Norcliffe inside at this moment? She found she had little desire to see him again, even after his unexpected offer of employment. He had certainly earned his infamous reputation. She tore her eyes away and hurried to catch Mrs. Morton.

They continued the tour upstairs, through a maze of hallways that Rose doubted she would ever keep straight. Every door began to look the same, and only her brief glimpses out the wide windows allowed her to keep her bearings. Mrs. Morton shot out words faster than anyone she'd ever met, and Rose's head throbbed in her attempt to remember everything.

"You'll rise at four o'clock every morning. Your duties include cleaning and setting the fireplace grates, sweeping all floors daily, dusting and polishing, helping in the kitchen, hauling water, and anything else I assign you." Mrs. Morton fixed her with a glare. "You will complete all your tasks by the end of the day or I will report your inadequacy to his lordship. Am I understood?"

"Yes, Mrs. Morton," she said, eager to please. The housekeeper turned away with a scowl.

After turning down another endless hallway, Mrs. Morton came to a halt outside an innocuous door, the same as all the others. She faced Rose with a severe expression.

"As a maid, you are expected to be invisible. Your presence will never be noticed, though you'll be in every room of the house." She laid her hand on the doorknob. "Every room except this one."

Rose glanced at the door again. "What room is that?"

Mrs. Morton's eyes took on a new solemnity. "It was the bedchamber of the late baroness."

Rose bit her lip. The sudden deaths of Lord and Lady Norcliffe in a carriage accident had shaken the entire town two years before.

"His lordship insists on privacy in this matter," Mrs. Morton said. "Only *I* am allowed inside to clean. You are never to enter this room."

Rose nodded. That would *not* be a problem. She had far too much depending on her ability to keep this position.

The tour finished in the attic, where Mrs. Morton showed Rose her sliver of a bedroom, furnished with a bed and tiny wash table.

"Fetch your things from downstairs." She eyed Rose from head to foot and gave a little scoff. "You'll have to accustom yourself to the livery. We've no use for frilly dresses."

Rose stared down at her dress as Mrs. Morton left. Frilly? The dark blue muslin was one of her plainer dresses. Heavens, she still had so much to learn. Her energy spent, she sank onto the bed, the iron frame creaking in the silence. She wrapped her arms around herself, clutching her elbows in a fierce effort to control her emotions.

What had she gotten herself into? Though surprised at Lord Norcliffe's offer yesterday, she hadn't needed more than a moment to accept the position. Even a post as an undermaid was vastly preferable to the uncertain future that had loomed before her. And in truth, it was a good position, and she had been confident she would be able to manage.

But now … oh, but now she was not so certain. Mrs. Morton had made it all too clear that she would report anything lacking in Rose's work. And the sheer amount of work! The house was enormous, and Rose would be lucky enough to not lose her way, let alone complete the tasks expected of her.

Rose closed her eyes, forcing back her tears of self-pity. She was lucky to have found this position, lucky to not be on the streets—or even worse, the workhouse. It would be difficult, of that she had no doubt. But she would learn and grow stronger.

Father was depending on her, and she would not let him down.

Henry did not particularly like his weekly meetings with Frampton and Mrs. Morton. His housekeeper had the tendency to drone on about useless details while his butler barely spoke at all. But in the absence of having a steward, the meetings had become a necessity. As Mrs. Morton spoke from across the desk, something about the rising price of candles, he resolved to double his search for a new steward.

"Would you like to review the menu for the week?" Mrs. Morton asked in that strange, toneless voice of hers.

Henry shook his head. "No, I haven't the time. As I said last week, I shall leave it to you to decide."

Mrs. Morton frowned, but nodded. With no lady of the house to confer with, she often attempted to involve him in such inane discussions. He hardly cared if they ate fish or fowl, so long as it was palatable.

Henry decided to cut the meeting short before Mrs. Morton could start into another endless dialogue. "If you have no other concerns, then—"

"I do have another concern," Mrs. Morton said quickly.

Henry narrowed his eyes at her interruption. She flushed but sat straighter. "Lord Norcliffe," she amended.

Henry tightened his jaw and looked out his study window, where the summer leaves were twitching in a scant breeze. He exhaled; the sooner he heard her concern, the sooner he might escape outside for a bruising ride. He motioned for her to speak.

"I am worried about the maid you hired, my lord," she said.

Henry leaned back in his chair. It was as though Mrs. Morton knew how often he'd thought of Miss Sinclair during the past week. It had been utterly foolish of him to hire her. What had he been thinking, mixing a debtor's daughter into his staff? Especially one with no experience.

"Is her work inadequate?" he asked.

Mrs. Morton frowned. "No, I can't say that it is, though she is slow. But my main trouble is how she is affecting the other servants."

Henry's first thought—an odd, irritating thought—was that the male servants were distracted by Miss Sinclair. He shook that away.

"She acts quite pretentious around the others," Mrs. Morton went on. "Takes her meals alone, stays aloof from everyone. I daresay she thinks herself above the rest."

"Has she said anything to that effect?" He drummed his fingers on his desk. He had no patience for household disputes.

Mrs. Morton clasped her hands in her lap. "Not precisely, but her general air is very off-putting."

Frampton, sitting beside Mrs. Morton, raised an eyebrow but said nothing.

Henry shook his head. "I can hardly dismiss someone for being 'off-putting'. As long as her work is satisfactory, I can see no issue." He closed his ledger book. "Mrs. Morton, you may leave. I've a matter to discuss with Frampton."

Mrs. Morton cast a suspicious glance between the two of them, but did not argue as she curtsied and left.

Henry leaned back in his chair. "Tell me the truth, Frampton. I do not wish for there to be contention belowstairs."

Frampton focused his aging eyes on Henry's. "My lord, you may have contention whether you wish it or not."

"Why is that?"

"The problem is not with Rose, but the other servants." He sighed. "Apparently one of the upper maids wished the open position to go to a younger sister and has spread resentment among the staff."

"What nonsense." The position was Henry's to give, and the fact that any of his servants thought themselves entitled to it irritated him to no end.

"I quite agree." Frampton cleared his throat. "I feel I should tell you I do not concur with Mrs. Morton's assessment of Rose. She says the girl is pretentious, but I see her as reserved. In the week she has been here, I have found her to be hard working and eager to please." He shook his head. "In truth, she smiles more than the rest of the household combined."

Henry could easily believe that, thinking of his meeting with Miss Sinclair when she had smiled so gratefully at him. But a smile was not the making of a good servant. "Loyalty and diligence rank much higher in my opinion of a good servant than a pretty smile."

"Then I hope she proves herself in time."

"As do I," Henry muttered. If Miss Sinclair did not succeed, he doubted he would ever see a penny of what her father still owed him.

Frampton nodded, but did not stand. Henry knew better than to think the conversation over. The butler had been a part of Norcliffe House as long as Henry could remember and he was well used to the man's unassuming nature. "What is it, Frampton?"

The butler frowned, the lines of his face heavy. "Charlie had an errand in town this morning. When he returned, it was with distressing news."

"What is that?"

"John Ramsbury has returned to the area."

Henry's chest tightened. He sat forward in his chair, his eyes focused on Frampton's. "You're certain?"

"Charlie heard it from the Ramsburys' cook herself."

"He's back, then." Henry's voice growled low in his throat. "No doubt coming to see if his father is close enough to death to expect an inheritance soon."

Frampton did not offer his opinion, but it was clear from his hard expression that he agreed. Henry shook his head, trying to ignore the heat flooding his veins. He had tried to put the past behind him, but it had clearly been a failed attempt. Even the thought of seeing John's face—his narrow smirk and calculating eyes—made his shoulders tense.

Frampton was still watching him. Henry set his jaw and met his butler's eyes again. "Thank you, Frampton."

Frampton rose and gave a bow, deeper than his usual stiff motion. It was his way of showing support, and Henry was grateful for the gesture. He had never needed it more.

John Ramsbury had returned. His closest friend, his trusted ally—and the man who had taken everything from him.

Chapter Three

Rose had never been so exhausted in all her life. She'd thought selling the bookshop's contents had been quite the task—taking inventory, packing the books, arranging their shipment to shops around the county. But even that chore paled in comparison to the drudgery she now experienced from the first light of dawn to the dark shadows of night.

Every waking hour of the last week had been spent in never-ending and draining tasks: sweeping every inch of the manor, dusting each surface, beating rugs for hours on end, washing windows, hauling buckets of water up and down stairs. Mrs. Morton made certain Rose had no chance to even catch a breath before assigning her a new undertaking. And every night, when the other maids finished their work—giving her smug glances as they passed—Rose worked on, scrubbing and polishing and trying very hard not to cry as the daylight faded.

Tonight was particularly difficult, though she could not say exactly why. Perhaps it was because her back hurt from the effort of bending over her fourth fireplace of the evening, or that her hands were cracked and sore from clenching the brush handle as she scoured and scrubbed the bricks. Or perhaps it was the aching beat behind her eyes that spoke of too little sleep.

But as she sat back against the edge of the fireplace to relieve the pain in her knees, she knew it was far more than that. It was the knowledge that this week had been the longest week of her life since Mama had died. If every week was to be as bone-wearying and demanding as this one, she did not know how she would survive.

Rose had done the equations. She was excellent at arithmetic, no matter how Lord Norcliffe doubted her abilities. At a maid's wage, and paying her father's prison fees, she would be working here for close to seven years. Seven years without any hope of promotion, approval, or friendship. Seven years without anything resembling happiness.

Sometimes she wished she wasn't so very good with numbers.

Rose rested her head against the cold brick of the fireplace, soothing the throbbing in her temples. She closed her eyes and wished that when she opened them again, she would be back in their cozy rooms above the bookshop, Papa reading aloud from their newest acquisition, warm cups of tea in their hands. Since she was dreaming of impossible things, she added Mama next to her on the settee, mending Papa's coat, an easy laugh on her lips.

If only her desperate imaginings could be as real as the cruel stone and choking darkness that surrounded her now.

The candles burned low throughout the drawing room, the evening creeping in the windows. Henry squinted at his book—a particularly dull text about farmland irrigation—and could not focus on the words. He exhaled and tossed the book on the table beside him. He could call a servant to bring more candles, but the dim light was rather a good excuse not to continue wading through such a tedious task.

Since his steward had left for another position to be closer to his ill mother, Henry had been utterly overwhelmed by the work left to him. He knew he needed to hire another steward, but trust came slowly to him. Mr. Turner had been his father's steward for over a decade; finding a suitable replacement would take time.

Henry stood, walking to the window and peering out into the darkness. He could see nothing but the barest outline of the trees, the sky a lighter shade of black. Turning back, he surveyed the empty drawing room: brocaded sofas, plush rugs and cushions, the enormous stone fireplace. Two letters lay on the writing desk in the corner, one from each of his older sisters, both inviting him to visit. He was sorely tempted; he missed his nephews and nieces, and his sisters, though they were several years his senior—and always keen to play matchmaker. But visiting them would also require that he step into

Society once more, and he was far from willing to do that.

In any case, he could hardly leave Norcliffe House now, not with his steward gone, Ramsbury returned, and Miss Sinclair making trouble belowstairs.

The silence and loneliness grew with every second, so he retrieved his book and left the room. The halls were dimly lit, as he'd ordered. No need to keep candles burning in every corridor when he was the only family member in residence.

Henry entered the library, striding toward where he had found the book earlier. Halfway there, he stopped. His shadow stretched long and spindly against the bookshelves lining the room. Where was that light coming from?

He turned. A figure sat on the floor—a maid. She leaned against the edge of the fireplace, a flickering candle beside her. The weak light played across her face; lips parted, eyes closed, her features soft.

He stepped forward, wanting to be sure he wasn't mistaken. But it *was* Miss Sinclair, so fast asleep she hadn't even heard him enter. What on earth was she doing here? The other servants would have finished their work long before. But she was still surrounded by buckets and brushes. Mrs. Morton had said she was slow, but he'd not expected to see her still working at nearly eleven o'clock.

Except she wasn't working; she was sleeping. He scowled. No matter her circumstances or inexperience, this was unacceptable. He drew closer, taking in her ash-covered dress and messy tendrils of dark hair. Nudging her with his boot seemed a bit low, even for a servant. In the end, he cleared his throat.

"Miss Sinclair." His voice pierced the quiet of the room. She started, her head snapping up, eyes blinking against the faint candlelight as she looked hazily about the room. Then her gaze froze on his boots, and slowly traveled up to meet his.

Her mouth dropped open and she scrambled to her feet. "Lord Norcliffe," she stammered, brushing off her skirts with frantic motions.

He clasped his hands behind his back, still holding his book, letting his disapproval show on his face. "I don't recall napping in my library to be among your duties."

"I am sorry, I did not mean to—" Her voice failed and she dropped into a wobbling curtsy. "I only closed my eyes for a moment. I promise I haven't done it before, I was just resting before finishing the other grates."

The panic in her eyes was real. Henry felt the tiniest bit of guilt, but he pushed it away. He was the master of the house. Why should he feel guilty for reprimanding his own servant?

"Mrs. Morton has told me you are slow in your work." His voice was cold and hard. "I did not realize how slow."

Miss Sinclair dropped her gaze and wrung her hands before her. "I am trying, my lord. And I am improving, I promise. This is only my fourth grate this evening. By the sixth, I'm certain I'll be something of an authority."

He raised an eyebrow. Most of his servants said nothing beyond "Yes, my lord." But not having been trained in service, Miss Sinclair did not understand she was running her tongue.

Then he realized what she had said. "You were assigned to clean six grates this evening?"

She met his eyes. "Yes, of course."

He knew nothing about the work of a maid, but cleaning six fireplaces in one evening seemed excessive, especially after a full day of work.

"You needn't worry about me finishing tonight," she said hastily. "I did this fireplace in half the time as the first." She paused. "Well, except for the napping."

Henry squinted at her. Was that a joke? She went on before he had a chance to decide.

"I'll be done with the rest of them in no time." She did not wait for his dismissal, bending to pick up her buckets. As she moved closer to the candlelight, he caught a glimpse of her hands for the first time. They were an angry red, cracked and dry.

"Your hands," he said without thinking. "What happened?"

Miss Sinclair inhaled sharply, straightening as she tucked her hands behind her. "Nothing, my lord."

It was clearly not nothing. Henry scrutinized her face, looking up at him with quiet determination, and understanding dawned. Her battered hands were a result of her work. She had been a shopkeeper's daughter before this, a life of relative comfort. She'd likely never known the hard labor of a servant. And yet not one word of complaint crossed her lips.

He fought the sympathy that rose inside him, tried to keep his thoughts objective. She was a servant now, and this was part of her life. She had accepted the post, hadn't she? It had been her choice.

Then why did he feel such accountability for the pain she was in?

"Go to bed." His words were gruff. "You may finish your work in the morning."

She stared at him. "My lord, I cannot. Mrs. Morton—"

"I will speak to Mrs. Morton," he said. "I'll not have you work yourself into illness. You'll be no use to me then."

She did not speak for a long moment. Her dark eyes were wide, shimmering in the candlelight. Or were those tears once again? "Thank you," she said in a soft voice.

His stomach gave a lurch at her words. He ignored it and gave a stiff nod, the issue settled. But instead of taking her things and leaving, Miss Sinclair stood still, watching him with a curious expression. She hesitated, glancing down to her feet, then back to his face. "What are you reading, my lord?"

He narrowed his eyes. The girl had no sense of propriety. He had given her a clear dismissal. "Techniques on farming irrigation," he answered shortly, certain his dull response would bring an end to this conversation.

"Are you enjoying it?"

Why should she care if he enjoyed his reading? "As much as anyone can enjoy such a subject."

She brushed back a lock of her dark hair, leaving a streak of ash across her cheek. "Why do you not read something you enjoy?"

"I cannot say I've ever enjoyed reading," he said. "I do not have the patience for it."

She gave a light laugh, contrasting strangely with the shadows under her eyes. "Then you are simply not reading the right books. I daresay I would dislike reading as well if I was forced to read about farming irrigation."

He tilted his head, scrutinizing her. "And what book would you recommend to me, then?" He couldn't say exactly why he was prolonging this conversation. It was hardly appropriate for them to be speaking at all. But the strangest curiosity rose inside him as he watched her. Miss Sinclair spoke to him as if it was perfectly natural, as if he was not a baron and she a maid. He could not decide if he liked the feeling or not.

She gave a little smile. "Oh, for you it shall have to be *Robinson Crusoe*. You'll not find your attention wandering with that tale, I am quite certain."

"You've read it?" he asked in disbelief.

She laughed again. "Do not be so very shocked. I read everything, even stories with cannibals and mutineers. It is—" Her voice cut out, and she cleared her throat. "That is, it *was* one of our more popular books at the shop."

The mention of her shop seemed to shake her, and she took a step back, fussing with the apron at her waist. "I am sorry, my lord, I should not blather on so. I'm sure you have much to do."

He opened his mouth, whether to reassure her or agree with her, he could not say. Before he could speak, she curtsied, took hold of her buckets, and ducked from the room, leaving him staring after her in bewilderment.

Chapter Four

Henry rose early the next morning, his meeting with Miss Sinclair still playing through his mind. He'd never had a more unusual conversation with a servant, though he found his thoughts lingering on her soft laugh and bright eyes as much as her words. Which was absolutely ridiculous, he told himself as he entered the stables, intent on a ride through the morning mist. He was simply unused to anyone speaking so freely with him; his servants generally scuttled about in a constant state of fear. Miss Sinclair certainly did not do that.

He left the stables in a trot, and when he reached the lawn he kicked his horse into a pounding gallop, hoping the cool air would rid his mind of such thoughts. He rode in the mornings as often as he could, when the world was still and quiet. Though Norcliffe House was secluded, there was always someone who needed him, whether it be Mrs. Morton, a tenant, or his ledger book. Out here in the woods, it was only him.

He reached the top of the nearest hill and pulled his mount to a stop. It was his favorite prospect of the estate. The trees spread thick and far, green in late summer, and farms dotted the spaces between. It looked the same as when he was a boy and yet it somehow looked different as well. Perhaps it was simply because he was different, changed by the passing of time.

Horse hooves sounded behind him. He turned to see a horse and rider stepping out from behind a stand of trees. Henry stiffened.

John Ramsbury. Of course it was him. Henry ought to have anticipated such an ambush. John knew his favorite rides, his favorite places. He would have found him sooner or later.

"Leave my land at once," Henry growled.

John did not look particularly alarmed at the less than friendly greeting. His face remained unaffected, his hair in that ridiculous Brutus style he favored. He stopped his mount a few paces away. "Is that how you greet your oldest friend?"

"It is how I greet any man who betrays my trust." Henry narrowed his eyes.

John held up his hands in surrender. "Please Henry, I did not come here in search of a fight."

"Then why did you come here?" He had no patience for this, not during what was supposed to be his solitary ride.

"To make amends," John said quietly. "You must know how much I regret what happened."

"Do you now?" Henry could barely contain the rage that simmered inside him. He clenched his reins so fiercely that he could feel his pulse in his fingertips.

"Of course I do." John ran his hand through his hair. "I tried to speak with you after the burial, but Frampton turned me away. I wrote you half a dozen letters trying to explain."

"You wrote me *one*." Henry gave a humorless laugh. "Did you think a letter could possibly make amends for what you did? You came to me with a preposterous scheme, which you claimed was a sound investment. 'Only a fool would turn it down' were your exact words, if I remember correctly, though there were more than enough fools involved from what I could tell."

"Henry—"

"And then," he said, louder, a dangerous edge finding his voice, "when I turned you down, knowing your history of terrible financial decisions, you waited until I left for London. You dared to approach my father with the same scheme, telling him I had approved the venture, when I certainly had not."

"And I wish every day that I hadn't." John leaned forward, his eyes intent on Henry's. "I swear, if I could change anything in my life, it would be that."

"You cannot." Henry's vision was spotting. Memory overtook reality—all he could see was Frampton's stricken face, the rain splattering against the windows. "You cared only for yourself and making enough money to pay your debts." His jaw tightened. "My mother and father died because of your selfishness."

John swallowed, for once having no answer. Because it was the truth, and he knew it. Frampton's words came back to Henry, echoing through his haze of anger. John had insisted Lord and Lady Norcliffe come immediately to London to see their new investment, despite an imminent storm and terrible road conditions. His parents had set out, excited at the undertaking, when their horses had been spooked by the storm. The coach was dragged down an embankment and into a river—and Henry's parents with it.

"I am sorry." John's voice was hoarse. "I truly am."

Henry shook his head. "I do not want your apologies."

John urged his horse a step closer. "Then let me tell you how I am trying to make it right."

"You cannot make it right." How could he even think that? Deluded, arrogant fool. He had used his connection to Henry to manipulate his parents, all for his own gain, and he thought an apology might fix things between them?

John sighed. "I know that. I only meant that I am trying to change myself, discover what my purpose should be."

"Being a careless fool was not enough of a goal?" Henry wished the man would rise to the insult, if only so their bout of words might change to a round of fisticuffs. He'd long wanted to drive his fist into John's smug, square jaw.

But John did not seem to hear the gibe. "I've found myself steady employment. You would be quite surprised at me, taking a position in trade. But I find a simple pleasure in it. I've been working to pay my debts." He paused, meeting Henry's eyes. "I've met a woman, the loveliest girl in London. I hope to propose marriage soon."

"And you want my blessing?" Henry asked scathingly. "I'm more likely to write her and warn her off."

"Come now, Henry." John shook his head. "It is impossible to change the past, but I am doing what I can to make amends. Will you hold a thoughtless mistake against me forever? Is our friendship worth so little to you?"

Henry tore his eyes away, glaring into the trees. Did John not understand that their friendship was what made his betrayal all the worse? When he remembered their years together—hiding from their nursemaids as boys, playing tricks on the teachers at Harrow, laughing their way across every ballroom in London—all he felt was pain.

He looked at John again, who waited in silence for Henry's judgment. He scrutinized the man, noting his simple clothing, his unremarkable mount. Had John truly lowered himself to work in trade? As the grandson of a marquess, he'd always claimed such work beneath him.

"Who is this girl you wish to marry?" he said, voice curt.

John straightened, his brow lifting. "Miss Dowding. She is lovely and kind, and generous to a fault."

"And she would take you, even with your debts?" Henry did not think any woman would be right in the head to take such a man as John. But love did strange things to a person—or so his sisters said.

"She would," John said. "Though her father is a bit more reticent."

"He would be a fool not to be." John Ramsbury was not what any man hoped for a son-in-law.

"True enough, though I hope to convince him." John spoke eagerly. "I am close to paying off my creditors, by next year if I manage carefully. But I can hardly ask Miss Dowding to wait for me, not with her father pressuring her to make a match." He paused, as if weighing a decision in his mind. "But if I had a loan—"

At his words, any traces of forgiveness flew out of Henry. "So that is why you are here." His anger from before was nothing compared to the seething rage that arose inside him now. "You come to me with your penitence, claiming you have changed, and still all you want is money."

"No, of course not!" John protested. "I am sincere, I swear. I don't care about the money."

"That is all you have ever cared about." Henry urged his horse forward. "Get off my land, Ramsbury, before I send for the constable."

John sent him one last look—though of pain or anger, Henry couldn't say—before he kicked his heels into his horse's flanks. Henry watched him race away, his teeth clenched so tightly he thought they would shatter.

He had let his guard down. He had almost been taken in once more, by the same man—a man who only brought grief and heartache.

He would not let it happen again.

Chapter Five

Rose paced at the bottom of the grand staircase, watching the front door with every turn of her feet. Even with her eyes on the door, she kept her hearing focused behind her. She knew Mrs. Morton would be cross if she found her standing about when she ought to be sweeping upstairs. But she had to speak to Lord Norcliffe. Even after only being here for a week, she knew his habits well, as all the servants did. He would be returning from his morning ride any minute.

She glanced down again at the letter, bent from her many readings in the last half hour since she'd received it. Her throat closed over and tears threatened yet again. Heavens, it felt like all she did these days was cry. What an exhausting business it was.

But she could hardly avoid it. Papa was ill, a cough and fever. This letter from his jailer explained that a doctor had been called to the prison to tend him, but her father needed extended care to recover. That meant more money, required immediately, of which she had none. That left her one option, reluctant as she was to take it. Lord Norcliffe.

Her conversation with the baron the night before had left her spinning—and mortified. Not only had he found her asleep in the library, but she had made quite the fool of herself chattering on about books. What had she been thinking, daring to make a recommendation to him? And then she had returned to her bedchamber to find streaks of ash across her cheeks, her hair a mess. No wonder he had sent her to bed. He likely thought her half mad from exhaustion.

But he *had* sent her to bed, for whatever reason. Kindness? Or was it as he claimed, to keep her healthy so she might continue to pay her father's debt? She was inclined to believe it was the former. The unexpected concern on his face when he had seen the state of her hands, his amusement at her attempt at conversation—was it possible there was some compassion behind his steely eyes and harsh voice?

She certainly hoped so, or this would be a very short meeting indeed.

Footsteps sounded behind her, and she turned. It was Mr. Frampton, the butler. She relaxed her rigid shoulders. Though she was shunned by the servants belowstairs, Mr. Frampton treated her the same as he did all the staff.

He approached now. "Are you lost again, Rose?"

She might have been offended that he thought her lost, standing there in the front entry, but seeing as he had found her quite turned around in the east wing not two days ago, she could hardly protest.

"I'm not lost," she said, clearing her throat. "I'm waiting. I need to speak with Lord Norcliffe straightaway."

"In regards to what?" Mr. Frampton's voice was wary, but at least he did not immediately send her on her way.

Rose took a deep breath, attempting to steady both her mind and heart. "My father is ill, and I've no money to pay for the physician's bills."

Was that a flash of sympathy in his eyes? "And you intend to ask his lordship for additional funds."

She nodded, expecting a reprimand, but he only frowned. "I see. Well, do not dawdle overlong; Mrs. Morton will still expect your chores to be finished in a timely manner." He continued down the hallway without another word.

His indifference did not bode particularly well, but then again, Mr. Frampton did not know about her encounter with Lord Norcliffe the night before. She had seen a glimpse of kindness in him and could only hope it was not a rare occurrence.

Footsteps came from outside, mounting the stairs. Rose's stomach leaped into her throat and she spun as the door was thrown open, silhouetting a tall figure against the morning sun. A footman hurried to catch the door, but Lord Norcliffe was already striding across the entry, yanking his gloves from his hands and tossing his hat onto a nearby table, his fair hair mussed from his ride.

Rose hurried forward, intent on catching him before he disappeared into his study. "Lord Norcliffe," she called.

He looked up and—far too late—Rose noticed his expression. His eyes burned, his jaw tight and his shoulders rigid under his riding jacket. She inhaled sharply, her stomach twisting.

"What now?" he snapped, coming to a halt.

She stared at him. What had put him in such a foul mood? She wished she could retreat, but his gaze narrowed on her, the silent tension growing every moment she hesitated.

"I—I am sorry to bother you," she stammered. "I wished to speak to you a moment."

He said nothing, motioning her to speak on with a pointed gesture, as if she was hardly worth his time. Which she likely wasn't.

Rose took a deep breath. "I've had a letter from my father's jailer with distressing news. I hoped to ask for—"

Lord Norcliffe gave a sharp laugh, and she stopped. "Oh, I know what you want," he said, stepping forward with a dangerous gleam to his eye. "You want what everyone wants from me. Money."

It took all Rose had not to stumble backwards, away from his accusing voice. "I didn't mean—that is, I only—" Her voice caught in her throat, an odd hum in her ears.

"I've had enough requests for today." His harsh voice echoed strangely in the high-ceilinged entry, and Rose's face flushed with heat, her hands shaking as she clutched her letter against her chest. "Leave my sight before I dismiss you altogether."

He stalked down the hall to his study and disappeared inside with a crash of his door.

Rose gaped after him. What had happened? She backed away, turning and hurrying to the servants' stairs. She dropped onto the bottom step, her breaths coming too fast as she pressed a hand against her stomach.

How had she misread him so badly last night? There had been no trace just now of the kindness she had seen in the library. She was a fool to think she could know a man in the span of a stolen conversation.

Rose shook her head; she could not dwell on it. She had to find a way to help her father, and she had to do it soon.

Chapter Six

Henry could not focus. He'd been trying since the day before to forget his meeting with John Ramsbury, but every time he closed his eyes, John's face mocked him, remorseful and yet completely deceitful.

He pushed back from his desk and went to the window, gazing out into the gloomy afternoon, clouds hanging low with the threat of rain. Though his anger had dissipated somewhat, he still could not settle his mind. He was restless, and pacing the halls of this great, echoing house did nothing to help. He leaned against the window frame, eyes unseeing as they skipped over the familiar landscape.

Movement caught his attention, and he squinted at a slim figure hurrying down the drive, dressed in a blue pelisse and bonnet. The woman glanced back, displaying her delicate features in profile. Miss Sinclair.

A new feeling rose inside him then, niggling past his pride and anger. He had been in a fuming haze when he'd returned from his ride yesterday, but he could still remember the shock in Miss Sinclair's eyes when he'd berated her in the entry. Shock—and fear.

But why should he care what she thought of him? She was his servant, nothing more. Shouldn't a servant fear her master? He crossed his arms, watching her figure as she walked down the lane, her movements graceful. He wished he could believe what he was telling himself, but the guilt that itched inside him spoke more truthfully than his own thoughts.

The door opened behind him and Frampton's reflection appeared in the window. "Today's post, my lord," he said, coming forward with a silver tray.

Henry hardly noticed, his eyes still upon Miss Sinclair. Where was she going anyway? Should she not be working? He attempted to rally his anger once more. "Where is Miss Sinclair going?" He gestured to the window as he turned to face Frampton.

Frampton looked unbothered by the force of the question. "I believe it is her half day."

Henry grunted, wishing his butler's response was not so logical.

"Did she have the chance to speak with you yesterday?" Frampton set his tray on the desk.

"You knew about that?"

"Indeed." He brushed his gloved hands together. "I found her quite distressed over the news of her father."

"Her father?" Henry furrowed his brow. Had she mentioned her father? All he could remember was her request for money, which had sent his anger boiling over. "What happened to her father?"

Frampton turned back to him. "He is quite ill, enough to send for a physician. His jailer demanded Rose pay the fees immediately. Did she not discuss this with you?"

Henry swallowed. "She attempted to." He turned back to the window. Miss Sinclair had disappeared past the brick pillars that marked the entrance to the estate, but her face appeared in his mind. Wide dark eyes, mouth parted in astonishment, skin pale as a ghost. She had been trying to help her father, and he had rejected her without a second thought.

For two years he'd carefully crafted his callous reputation, depending on it to guard against those who would exploit him. It was his best means of protecting himself. But he never realized how it might hurt someone. Someone innocent of ill-intentions.

What would his mother think of what he had done?

He hesitated a moment more before he turned and strode to the door. "Have my horse readied immediately," he called back to Frampton.

Rose shivered and pulled her pelisse more tightly around her. Even in late summer, the grey clouds and stiff breeze held a chill that crept through her layers. She touched her neck, making certain Mama's necklace still hung safely there. It had been silly, wearing it instead of tucking it inside her reticule. But as this would be her last chance, she could not stop herself.

Her mother's necklace was the only item of value she had left after selling all her possessions to pay Papa's debts. She ached to think of parting with it, but what choice did she have after her disastrous attempt with Lord Norcliffe? Even now, the memory of his harsh eyes and even harsher words sent a wave of anxiety through her.

She'd been walking a quarter hour when hoofbeats sounded behind her. She moved to the side of the road to let the other traveler past, glancing up as the horse came even with her. She stopped in her tracks, staring up at the rider.

"Lord Norcliffe," she sputtered. He looked down on her with an unreadable expression, looking far too at ease on horseback. She remembered to curtsy, though it was so unsteady it hardly counted.

"Miss Sinclair." He dismounted, taking his horse's reins as he stepped toward her. "Might I join you?"

"I—" She couldn't seem to catch her breath. He wished to walk with her? "Yes, of course."

He gestured her forward. She somehow managed to convince her feet to move, and he fell in step beside her. Nerves preyed upon her mind. Why was he here? Perhaps he had decided to dismiss her after all. But why would he wait until she had left the house?

"Miss Sinclair," he said in a gruff voice. "I wanted to … apologize for my behavior to you the other day."

She blinked. "Apologize?"

"Yes." He cleared his throat. "I was upset about another matter and treated you poorly when you had done nothing wrong."

She shook her head, twisting her gloved fingertips. "I should apologize to *you*, my lord. I promised when you took me on that I would make no more requests of you, and then I came asking for another favor."

"A favor that was not for you."

Rose peeked sideways at him, attempting to read his expression. He did not look at her and kept his eyes straight ahead on the road.

"It *was* for me," she said quietly. "My father is all I have."

He looked at her then, his eyes intent as they scrutinized her face. "Frampton says your father is ill."

She nodded, trying hard not to show how worried she was. "Yes, my lord. I would go to him myself, but—" She stopped, dropping her gaze. What a foolish thing to say. "That is, of course I would not leave my post now."

Lord Norcliffe looked away. "Have you found a way to pay his fees?"

Why would he ask that? Was this a change of heart? She had trouble believing it, considering how he had reacted yesterday. Her hand went to her necklace and traced the familiar shape of the golden rose with her fingers. "I have a plan, yes."

His eyes followed her movement and fixed on her necklace. Her stomach jolted, realizing how it must look to him. She had come to him pleading for money, and here she was wearing a necklace that, while surely not extravagant to him, was quite unnecessary for a girl of her current station. Did he wonder why she hadn't sold it before now?

"It was my mother's," she blurted, grasping the chain tightly in her hand.

His brow furrowed. "Pardon?"

"This necklace," she said. "It was my mother's. And my grandmother's before her. They were also named Rose."

"I see," he said, though he did not look as though he understood at all, watching her in perplexity. "A family heirloom."

"Er, yes." Did he not care how valuable it was? Or had he not yet made the connection? "It is all I have left of my mother."

"You must be quite attached to it."

"I—I suppose." Rose let her hand drop to her side, toying with her reticule on her wrist. "It helps me to remember her." She hated the thought of selling it, but her father's life meant more than any trinket, no matter its memories.

"I understand the sentiment," he said. She turned her head to look at him in surprise. He looked just as surprised at his own words. The slightest hint of pink touched the angles of his cheeks. "That is, becoming attached to an item. There is more value to an object that is associated with a loved one."

She watched him for a long moment before replying. "You speak from experience," she said slowly. "Not observation."

His jaw tightened. "Yes." His voice was short, but not rude.

"What thing do you value?" She wasn't certain why she pressed him. There was just a look about the baron that she could not quite name. A mix of loneliness and pride, perhaps. But she should try and keep her words to herself. He had proven himself unpredictable, and she was not anxious to be shouted at again.

He did not speak for a long moment and Rose fidgeted with the edges of her pelisse. He clearly thought her too forward. But then he spoke.

"My father gifted my mother a beautiful gold hand mirror at their wedding." His eyes were distant in remembrance. "She was quite sentimental about it and I must have seen it every day of my life. I haven't had the heart to move it from her vanity, not since …"

His voice drifted off, pain filling his expression. Mrs. Morton's words came back to her, the warning not to enter the late baroness's rooms, and now Rose realized why. Lord Norcliffe kept his memories there, like a flower pressed between the pages of a book. She wanted to reach out, touch his arm or speak a kind word, but her voice abandoned her. How did one comfort a man she barely knew? Especially her own employer.

The wind began to blow more fiercely against her face, but she hardly noticed as she sorted through her thoughts.

"I think it is good to have such a reminder of your mother," she finally said. "Memory fades so quickly." Her own mother's face had grown hazy in her mind. What she would not give for a miniature of her mother, to better remember her laughing eyes and kind smile.

He nodded and they walked again in silence, though more comfortable than before. Rose's shoulders relaxed slightly. She was beginning to think that this man—this thoughtful, perceptive man—was more the reality of who Lord Norcliffe was than the one who had shouted at her. But why was there such a difference to begin with? Why had he acted like such a beast if there was another man entirely inside of him?

"Do you have an errand in town?" he asked, filling the quiet. "Or a visit perhaps?"

She touched her necklace again. "An errand, yes." A small part of her wished to tuck away her pride and ask Lord Norcliffe once again for help. But she did not want to risk their tentative peace. "And you, my lord, do you have business in town?"

The pleasantries felt odd after the depth of their conversation. He opened his mouth to speak—but a drop of rain hit his cheek. A moment later, one splashed on her arm, and then one after another until the rain fell in a resounding chorus all around them. Rose inhaled sharply and clasped her bonnet to her head. She hadn't realized the storm clouds were so close.

"Blast it all." Lord Norcliffe turned, his eyes searching in all directions as the rain fell harder, soaking his shoulders and dripping off his topper. "We must find shelter."

Rose blinked the rain from her eyes. Shelter? They were still miles from town.

Lord Norcliffe met her eyes, his expression resolved. "There's an old gamekeeper's cottage not far from here." He had to raise his voice as the wind began to howl.

Her pelisse was already damp and she jumped as distant thunder rolled through the wooded hills. She managed a nod.

"It will be quicker if we ride," he said briskly. "Come, I'll help you up."

She gaped at him. "Ride?" Did he mean together?

"Yes, of course. Unless you wish to catch your death?"

His abruptness did nothing to quell the anxiety that swelled in her. She rode but rarely, and never with another person. But he waved her forward impatiently as the rain continued to pelt them. She joined him beside the horse. Heavens, but it was tall. She glanced around for a log to serve as a mounting block.

"Shall I—"

His hands came around her waist and she was lifted into the air before she could utter a gasp. He settled her sideways on the saddle as she gawked at him, but he wasted no time in pulling himself up behind her.

"No time for propriety," he murmured in her ear, slipping one arm around her waist. Her back was pressed against him, lighting a strange heat in her chest. He kicked his horse and Rose only had a moment to grasp the saddle before they were dashing through the rain.

Chapter Seven

Was that her heart beating rapidly in her ears, or just the sound of the horse's hooves pounding into the damp ground? If it *was* her heart, Rose could only hope the sound was drowned out by the rain and wind. What would Lord Norcliffe think if he knew how affected she was by his strong arms around her, the commanding ease with which he directed his horse?

He said not a word as they rode, rain pouring down around them. Despite the speed at which they raced across the countryside, his hold on her was tight and she felt no fear.

A small, stone cottage came into view, nestled between two chestnut trees. Lord Norcliffe pulled his mount to a stop and dismounted, splashing into the mud. Rose shivered. She hadn't realized how warm he had been against her, shielding her from the wind. She unclenched her hands from the saddle and looked down at the ground in apprehension. But again, the baron did not stop to ask for permission. He reached up and took her by the waist, his movements effortless as he slid her to the ground.

He took the horse's reins. "Come," he called through the deluge. She hurried after him, following the horse up onto a wide, covered porch. He tied his mount's reins to a beam, patted the horse's flank apologetically, and then ushered Rose inside the front door.

She moved into the cottage, clutching her arms about herself as she shivered. The space was dark and dank; the windows were boarded up, letting in hints of light. Water dripped from the roof, which clearly had not been repaired in years.

Lord Norcliffe stepped in behind her. She turned and then froze, her eyes fixed on him as he removed his hat. His light hair was darkened by the rain, dripping and splayed across his forehead, his sharp jawline emphasized by the color in his face, from the cold or the exercise, she couldn't say. And his eyes were vibrant, alive. She ought to look demurely away, but found it quite impossible.

"I wish I could offer better accommodations," he said.

It is fine, her mind told her to say. *A roof is enough.*

Instead, in some mad fit of humor, her mouth let loose a short laugh. She clasped a hand to her lips, but the perplexed look on his face only made her laugh again, harder and without any restraint.

"I am—" She stopped, laughter still bubbling up inside. "I am sorry," she finally managed, her mouth unable to stop smiling. "I don't mean to imply this is humorous at all."

"Your laughter would indicate otherwise." His words were reproachful, and yet, to her astonishment, one corner of his mouth twitched.

"I don't mean to laugh." She reached up and untied her bonnet, shaking the rain from its brim. She hoped it would dry properly. "It's just that this seems like an incident from one of Mrs. Radcliffe's novels, a handsome baron rescuing a damsel from the rain."

He raised an eyebrow. "Handsome?"

Heat flamed across her face and she stared at him with wide eyes. "I mean—that is I *meant*—that the heroes in her novels are always handsome—"

"So you *don't* find me handsome then?"

She took a deep breath, thoughts tumbling through her mind. What possible answer could she give to that?

But then he grinned, a crooked smile that was entirely at odds with their interactions so far. His eyes were alight with mischief.

"You should not tease me so," she scolded. "I am in no position to know whether you are in earnest or not."

He crossed his arms. "It hardly matters since you speak candidly regardless of the situation."

She *was* a bit outspoken. "I am sorry. I will try harder to be more reserved in the future."

"And why would I wish that?" he asked, squinting at her in the dim light.

"A servant is not employed for her opinions." Speaking the word *servant* reminded her how absurd this situation was. In all the turmoil of the storm, she'd almost forgotten who she was—who *he* was. Her hands went to the mess that was her hair, smoothing back her drenched curls.

"No, but I do tire of the bowing and scraping. A bit of straightforwardness is refreshing." He paused. "And I admit I have difficulty thinking of you as a servant."

Was that good or bad? He looked at her through narrowed eyes, though not in anger or irritation. Rather as though he was trying to remember a time he had seen her before, but could not place it.

The look was gone in the next moment. He turned, inspecting the interior of the cottage. "I imagine we'll be caught here for a while yet."

"Then it is good you do not seem to mind my loose tongue."

His mouth twitched. "Indeed. The afternoon would pass terribly slow if you were too frightened to speak to me."

"Which is no small thing, since you seem quite determined to frighten everyone away."

The humor in his eyes slipped. "Pardon?"

She caught her breath; she should not have said that. But her tongue had run wild, drawn into this conversation without any thought. She could not take back her words, so she took a steadying breath and pressed on. "I simply cannot take your measure, my lord. One moment you are generous, offering me a position, and the next—"

"I am shouting at you."

"Well, yes." She swallowed. "And I cannot decide which side of you is the true side, though I have little doubt you wish everyone to believe you are nothing more than an irritable man not to be crossed."

He clasped his hands behind his back and did not respond. Was he angry? She could not tell from his impassive expression. She dropped her gaze, tugging anxiously on her damp gown. "I apologize, my lord. I mean no offense."

There was a long minute of silence, and she dared not look up. His voice was gruff when he spoke next.

"I've had far too many people attempt to manipulate me for my wealth and title." He shook his head. "Since my parents' deaths, I find keeping the world at arm's length the best way to avoid them, and being 'irritable,' as you say, helps me achieve the peace that I want."

Rose examined him, his eyes distant. "That sounds rather lonesome to me."

He gave a sharp laugh. "Better to be lonely than used."

Used? There must be more to this story than he was telling her, but she could hardly force it out of him. "Perhaps you simply are not friends with the right sort of people. The world is not so terrible as all that."

He squinted at her. "I do not know how you can believe that, considering your lot in life."

She lifted one shoulder. "I've learned that although I have no influence over the decisions of others, I can choose how I respond. Bitterness will not help, and I am determined not to waste my time with it."

He stared at her. "I've never met anyone like you, Miss Sinclair."

"I am your servant," she reminded him. "You may call me Rose."

His eyes lingered on her face, and a shiver ran across her skin, though she was certain it was not because of the cold. "Again, I have quite the difficulty thinking of you as a servant."

Her stomach fluttered. What *did* he think of her then? She turned away, going to sit upon the ledge beside the window. "That is likely because I am not terribly good at being a servant. I am far too frank and far too slow, as you are well aware."

He followed her lead, though he sat on the window ledge across the cottage, far enough to allow the appearance of propriety, but still close enough to speak. "And were you much better at being a shopkeeper's daughter?"

"Oh, I was excellent at it," she said firmly. "I loved it, really. Papa allowed me the run of the shop, and I organized it to my heart's content. I could tell you where any book was at any time. I managed our finances the same way. I knew where every penny of our money went."

"How—" His voice broke off. He seemed not to know how to phrase his question.

"How did my father lose all our money without my knowing?" she offered.

He nodded and she sighed. "Papa began gambling after my mother's death. But I had no idea the problem had grown to this extent." She shook her head. "We had been planning to expand into a circulating library for years. I was saving for it, little by little. He did not tell me he was seeking investors, and whatever loans he received he used to pay his growing gambling debts. Eventually his creditors caught up to him." The image of Papa being taken away was forever branded into her memory.

She brushed a hand over her damp skirt, smoothing the wrinkles that creased the fabric. "He acted foolishly, I have no false ideas of that. But he is still my father."

"You have forgiven him?" There was no lack of skepticism in his question.

"Of course," she said. "I love him."

Lord Norcliffe was watching her again, brow furrowed. "I cannot say I find forgiveness to be as simple as you do."

She bit her lip, considering his words. "It depends entirely on the situation, I'm afraid. I can be quite stubborn as well."

"I'd not noticed," he said dryly.

Rose grinned. She rather liked Lord Norcliffe—at least when he wasn't yelling at her. Their conversation flowed easily, and she could not help her growing curiosity. He was determined to keep himself secluded from the world, and yet the way he spoke so freely with her made her think he was lonelier than he would ever admit.

Perhaps isolation was not truly what he wanted. Perhaps what he needed was a friend.

Chapter Eight

Henry was certain something was addled in his head. Two days had passed since his afternoon in the gamekeeper's cottage with Rose Sinclair, and still he could not go more than five minutes without thinking of her. He was nearing the end of his morning ride and he pushed his mount, urging the stallion up a steep incline, but he could not outrun his mind. His thoughts flashed continually through their conversation, which had bounded between topics like a hound on the hunt. Rose never allowed an uncomfortable silence, continually asking him questions.

They'd been confined to the cottage for nearly three hours as the rain fell steadily around them, yet Henry would have sworn it was not a half hour. When the wind finally calmed and the rain slowed to a drizzle, he accompanied her back to the road and watched her depart again for town with a feeling akin to disappointment. Rose's openness and sincerity awakened something inside him, a remnant of the man he'd been before his parents' accident. Once, he had been charming and witty. Once, he would never have thought twice about speaking to a beautiful woman.

That must be it, he decided as he slowed his horse to a walk, approaching Norcliffe House. It had simply been too long since he had conversed with a woman, save for his own tenants and household.

Except she *was* a part of his household. Why could he not remember that? Why was it that every time he came across Rose, he forgot who she was and what her father had done? He only saw her smile, bright and kind, and her arresting brown eyes that danced with an amused glimmer.

He shook his head, as if the motion might free him from his memories. He focused his gaze ahead as they approached his home. His eyes were drawn immediately to a figure standing at a second-floor window—Rose. She was holding the parlor draperies away from the window, inspecting them with such concentration that she did not notice him watching her from below.

Henry's stomach gave a strange lurch as she turned and left his view. She was likely alone in the parlor, amidst the mountain of chores given her by Mrs. Morton. He really ought to talk to his housekeeper about Rose's workload. Her dislike for Rose was obvious, probably stemming from their differences in background. Mrs. Morton had come to Norcliffe House from the Ramsbury household four years ago after having spent her entire life in service there, whereas Rose had lived a more privileged life. But he needed to ensure his housekeeper did not treat Rose unfairly.

He left his horse at the stables and walked up to the house, handing his hat and gloves to a footman at the front entrance. He went to his study, but paused with his hand on the knob. The knowledge that Rose was above him in the parlor set him on edge. He hadn't so much as seen her since the rainstorm.

Perhaps if he simply checked on her, made certain she hadn't caught a cold from being wet, then his mind could settle and he could get on with his day.

He climbed the stairs and walked down the hall, where the parlor door stood open. He stopped in the doorway and peered inside. Rose had dragged a tall stool to the window and balanced precariously on the top step. She was fiddling with the tops of the curtains, trying to release them from their holdings. A soft sound reached his ears, low and melodious.

Rose was humming.

He swallowed. Even as she worked to pay a debt she did not incur, to save the man who had, she was *humming*. He moved forward, entranced by not just the music, but by the way her dark hair escaped her bun, teasing the base of her neck, and how her figure curved beneath her dress as she bent her head to look under the curtains.

She stopped humming as he came up behind the stool. Instead, she placed her hands on her hips with a noise of frustration.

"How have the curtains earned your ire?" he asked without thinking.

She jolted, tipping the stool off balance. She threw out her arms with a yelp, but it was too late. Blood surged in Henry's head, and he sprang forward as she toppled off the stool, catching her in his arms with a soft thump.

Her eyes met his, wide with shock, and her lips parted as she stared at him, their faces inches apart. He stared back; he could not stop himself. Her smooth skin was flushed with pink, dark hair loose about her face, her slender frame pressed against his chest.

"My lord," she stammered. She scrambled to find her feet, moving away from him. She brushed her skirts and touched her hair, breathing fast. His own breaths were coming quicker than they ought.

She met his eyes. "My lord," she said again, but this time in a scolding voice. "What were you thinking, frightening me like that?"

When was the last time he had been scolded? Likely by his sisters for not visiting enough. And certainly not by his own servant. He ought to be irritated, but instead he found himself fighting the twitching in his lips.

"I am sorry," he said. "But I am not completely to blame. You are surprisingly unobservant, Miss Sinclair."

"Rose," she corrected. "And it is not among my duties to be observant. I am only charged with washing these drapes, which is proving more challenging than I thought."

"Might I offer my help?" What was his tongue doing? He did not have time to help maids with their work; he had enough paperwork piled on his desk to occupy his time for a solid week.

She shook her head and turned back to the stool. “I have things well in hand, my lord.”

“Clearly,” he said, amused. “And call me Henry.”

Her head jolted to look at him again, her surprise nearly matching his own. How had those words escaped his mouth?

“You know I cannot call you that,” she said.

He cleared his throat. “If I can call you Rose, then you may certainly call me Henry.” He moved forward to the stool and she backed away as he climbed.

“It is different,” she protested. “You are the master of the house. If anyone were to hear me—”

“Then do not let anyone hear you.” He was pleased to see pink spread across her cheeks. He turned back to the window, tugging the rod loose from the carved supports and lowering the curtains to the floor.

“Thank you.” He could tell she tried to speak grudgingly, but a smile teased at the corner of her lips.

“You are welcome,” he said as he stepped off the stool. “It is my house, after all. Am I to be excluded entirely from its running?”

“Most would think it strange that you would want to be involved.”

“And what would you think?”

Her dark eyes traveled across his face. “I daresay it is a unique quality in a baron. But certainly admirable.”

Her gaze did not leave his, and Henry suddenly felt vulnerable, as if she might look too deep into his mind and see what he was thinking about her. Because he should certainly *not* be thinking about how she was of the perfect height for him to kiss her. No, he should not be thinking that at all.

She saved him from his internal struggle. "Did you come to speak to me about something?"

He cleared his throat. "I came to see if you were recovered from our bout in the rain."

She smiled, that fascinating smile that made him wish to brush his thumb along her cheek. "It would take more than a bit of rain to dampen my spirits, sir."

"Sir" was better than "my lord" but he found himself wondering what his name would sound like from her lips.

"Good," he said, and then could think of nothing else to say. They had spoken easily before, trapped by the rain, with no constraints on their time or worries they might be overheard. With the house looming around them, and the knowledge that any number of servants might come upon them, he found his voice quite disappeared.

Rose did not allow for any gaps in their conversation. "It's a bit odd to talk in the house, isn't it?" She spoke in a low voice, her eyes crinkled at the corners. "After …"

"Yes," he said quickly. "I can't say I've ever conversed so freely with anyone in my household. I am not quite sure how to go about it."

"Well, I do not generally converse with barons, but I seem to be managing nicely."

He gave a short laugh, surprising himself. He could not remember the last time he had truly laughed. She was just so unexpected; he could never guess what she might say or do. In his life of order and regularity, she was like a sudden breeze, a wind of change that whispered of possibilities. For the briefest of moments, he imagined he saw something in her eyes, a flicker of something much deeper than amusement. But she turned away, brushing her hands on her apron.

"Unfortunately," she said, "despite my friendship with nobility, I still must wash these curtains and dust the room and polish the silver."

The spell was broken, the remembrance of their situation crashing down. She was a maid, and he was a peer of the realm. He could not allow his mind to imagine anything beyond that.

But was friendship beyond his capabilities? Could he not see this as a chance to become more like his father, who had known everything about his staff and house? In fact, now that he knew Rose better, he was quite convinced that her skills were being entirely wasted on menial chores. An idea flashed through his mind, one that felt perfect from conception.

"It just so happens," he said slowly, "that I have a different task for you, if you are willing to abandon your hard-won victory against the curtains."

She looked up at him in curiosity. "And what would that be?"

"You may have noticed that my library is horribly unorganized," he said. "It would be a perfect match of your talents if you would take the project on."

Her eyes widened. "Truly?"

"Truly," he said. "I should like you to start immediately. I'll speak to Mrs. Morton, and have another servant come and finish your tasks here."

Rose bit her lip and looked away. "I am not sure this is the best idea. I would hate to receive any special treatment. I do not think Mrs. Morton will like it."

He narrowed his eyes. "As this is my house, I hardly care what Mrs. Morton will think." In fact, it irked him that his servants might be more afraid of Mrs. Morton than of him. Though Rose was certainly not the average servant.

Still she hesitated, staring down at her shoes. "It is not just Mrs. Morton. I am an undermaid. I ought to be scrubbing floors, not organizing books. The other servants dislike me as it is, and I should not like to deepen their loathing of me."

For the first time, Henry realized how lonely she must be. Her only family, her father, was locked away for years, and she was isolated from the rest of the staff. She likely hadn't had much more conversation in the past fortnight than he had. He had little doubt that in time she would win over the other servants, but not if he elevated her, treated her differently. They would not forgive that of her.

He frowned. "I understand."

She nodded and began to turn away. But he could not give up so easily.

"Perhaps," he started, and she paused, "we might find a compromise."

She raised an eyebrow. "How so?"

He clasped his hands behind his back. "The fact is, I need my library organized, and I should like for you to do it. I will tell Mrs. Morton that you will take charge of the project, but that I understand I cannot take you from all your usual duties. Perhaps the mornings for the library, and the rest of the day relegated to your other tasks."

Rose pressed her lips together, her eyes impossible to read. They were normally wide, displaying her every emotion. But now they searched his face, intent and discerning.

"Are you certain?" she asked. "I would hate to be a nuisance."

Of course she would. Because she was far too kind for her own good.

"I am certain," he said firmly.

She nodded. "Then I would be glad to." She smiled, lighting her face and eyes, her lips curved into a tempting arc.

And Henry knew he was in very real trouble.

Chapter Nine

Were all barons so peculiar? Rose was inclined to believe that Henry—Lord Norcliffe—was quite the exception.

How many men of wealth and privilege would bother to spend most of their mornings in the company of a maid? But every morning for a fortnight, as she began her work in the library, organizing and cleaning, he found her. He brought along his ledger books and claimed a table in the corner for himself. They worked alongside each other, quiet at times, but often in earnest conversation. They spoke of so many things Rose could hardly keep them straight. They discussed their educations—he at Harrow and Cambridge, she at a girls' boarding school—and their families and childhoods, which were not so different, considering their difference in status.

"Do you think it odd," she asked him one morning, as she lifted a stack of books onto the table, "that we have never met before?" She could remember catching glimpses of the late Lord and Lady Norcliffe in town over the years, but never any of their children.

"Not terribly odd, no," he said from where he sat drafting a letter. "My family was often in London."

"I suppose," she said. "But perhaps we met as children and we simply cannot recall."

He looked up from his letter. "I sincerely doubt I ever met you before. I would have remembered."

She glanced away, hoping he did not notice the heat claiming her cheeks. She had a difficult time reconciling this man with the surly one she had first met in his study. Now he looked quite at ease, sitting there as if he had not a care in the world, though she knew he had more than a few pressing matters, acting as steward of his own estate. She could not bring herself to feel guilty about his time spent with her, however. He seemed to enjoy their talks as much as she did.

And she enjoyed them very much.

When he spoke in that deep, even tone of his—of his sisters and parents, the escapades of his nephews—she was transported from the feeling of entrapment that settled on her so easily. Her determination to see things through with a smile was challenging to keep up all the time. She'd had no more word from Marshalsea since she'd sent the money she'd earned from selling her necklace, and her worry grew with every passing day. But her mornings with Henry brought light into her darkening world, reminding her of all she had left and all she must continue to work to save.

In the moments of quiet, she stole glances at him, trying to piece together the puzzle that was the

Baron Norcliffe. Even with his sharp jaw and angled cheekbones, his face now looked softer somehow. Likely because he did not wear the perpetual scowl he'd sported the first few times they had met. And his blue-grey eyes were not so shadowed as they were before. In fact, they were lightest when they rested upon her.

Which was quite often. For as many times as she stole looks at him, he seemed to watch her just as much. Each time their eyes collided, she smiled and looked away, though it left her insides tilted, as if she was about to again fall from a stool.

You are being ridiculous, she scolded herself. *You are not a schoolgirl*. There was no possible way the baron looked at her with anything but friendship in mind. He was simply glad to find someone to talk to, to relieve the painful absence of his parents. If her company helped him find his way from that hole of grief, she would gladly do what she could.

However, their sunlit mornings could not last forever. Henry always had meetings with tenants and crops to oversee, and she had Mrs. Morton's endless list of chores after her time in the library each day.

Tonight was a particularly trying task: scrubbing the expansive floor of the portrait gallery. When she finally stood at the end of the hall, stretching her back and wincing at the pain in her knees, she felt a pride in her work. Even if she did it to pay a debt, it was good to do a job well.

She collected her rags and bucket, filled with brown, sloshing water, and made her way belowstairs. Laughter and conversation drifted from the servants' hall, which she tried to ignore. She did not think that being assigned to the library had caused any further issues, but the household staff—save for Frampton—still treated her as if she had a particularly contagious disease. Perhaps in time they would soften toward her, once they realized she was there to stay. It was not as though she had taken up this position on a curious whim. She sincerely needed both the money and the stability.

She stepped outside into the cool evening air and went to dump her bucket in the courtyard behind the house. Then she set it down and sighed, moving farther out into the night, her eyes going to the sky overhead where the first stars pierced the gray-black. She spent a few minutes of silence there, relishing the quiet and wishing she did not have only a dull, cramped bedroom to return to.

As she turned to go inside, she heard a noise, a whisper in the dark. It was a woman's voice, from around the corner of the house. Footsteps moved closer, and then another voice answering, deep and unmistakably male.

Rose did not want to eavesdrop, but neither did she wish to have any sort of contact with another servant at the moment. She did not particularly care for scathing looks and mocking smiles. She slipped behind the wash house, set away from the manor, and waited for the voices to pass.

Instead, they grew louder, stopping quite close to her.

"We have to do it soon," said the man's voice. "As soon as possible."

Rose did not recognize the voice, though that was hardly peculiar, considering how many servants were employed at Norcliffe.

"This cannot be rushed." The woman's voice was brusque and cool, one Rose *did* know. Mrs. Morton. "I must make certain everything is in place to deter his suspicion."

"Of course. We cannot compromise your position here. You are far too valuable." The man's tone was smooth, slipping over his words like butter on hot bread. "But the longer we wait, the greater the chance he will move it."

What on earth were they talking about? Who was suspicious, and what was being moved? Uneasiness rose inside her, and she tried to push it away. Surely it was none of her concern. And yet, why were they being secretive, meeting out here in the dark?

Mrs. Morton was silent for a long moment before answering. "Very well." She lowered her voice, muttering a few words that Rose could not make out. She leaned forward, as if the distance of a few inches might allow her hearing to reach, but to no avail.

"Excellent," the man said. Rose could almost hear the smile in his voice. "A pleasure, as always, Mrs. Morton."

Footsteps sounded as the man left, and Rose waited, certain Mrs. Morton would go inside and join the other servants. But Mrs. Morton's steps grew louder, coming in the direction of the washhouse that Rose now hid behind.

Her pulse jumped inside of her. Whatever Mrs. Morton and the stranger had been discussing, it had not been anything they wanted overheard. She grabbed up her bucket and hurried a few steps away, acting as if she had just emptied it.

Mrs. Morton turned the corner and stopped short. "Miss Sinclair," she barked.

Rose turned, forcing a look of surprise. "Mrs. Morton."

She could barely see the housekeeper's face by the light from a nearby window, but there was no denying the distrust in her eyes. "What are you doing? You can't have finished the gallery yet."

Rose kept her eyes wide and innocent, though she did not have to pretend the tremor in her voice. "Only just. Came to empty my bucket."

Mrs. Morton harrumphed. "I'll be inspecting it tomorrow. If I find your work lacking …"

Her voice drifted off, the threat so familiar to Rose by now that she did not even bother to worry over it. What frightened her most was the hard look in Mrs. Morton's eyes, beyond the usual dislike.

"I'll look it over again tonight," Rose managed, dropping her eyes.

Mrs. Morton sniffed and strode away. Rose let out a short breath, her heart beating furiously as if it had stopped during the entirety of the conversation.

Had she convinced Mrs. Morton that she had not overheard anything? She was hardly a talented actress, though her fear had been real. Mrs. Morton and the silver-tongued man were planning something, and certainly nothing innocent, or they would not need to meet in shadowy corners of the estate late at night.

What should she do? The first thought in her mind was to tell Henry. Except she had nothing substantial to tell. They had given no details or even said anything that might paint them as particularly suspicious. But the feeling that twisted in her stomach—a cold, dark sensation—signaled that something was not right. And Henry ought to know if something was not right in his home.

Chapter Ten

Henry eyed the gathering clouds as he strode down the main street in town. No matter how pleasant it had been the last time he had been caught in a rainstorm, he had no intention of doing it again. Especially since Rose was nowhere nearby. Hardly worth the nuisance of getting wet if she was not there.

He grinned at the memory, and two ladies standing outside the milliner's stared at him as he passed, no doubt shocked at the sight of Lord Norcliffe without a scowl. Rose was going to be terrible for his reputation, he could tell. But he could not bring himself to care very much.

He was turning to cross the street when his gaze fell upon the window of Fenton's Secondhand Shop. He froze, his eyes fixed upon a delicate gold necklace, the pendant an unmistakable shape of a rose.

That was Rose's necklace, the one she'd showed him on their walk. He would bet his estate on it. What was it doing in this window? It took a second longer for his mind to make the connection, flashing back to their conversation. She had *sold* it. She had sold the only thing she had left of her mother. All to pay for her father's medical fees, the ones Henry had refused to cover.

Henry stared at the necklace. How could such a woman as Rose exist? How could she be so selfless, so kind? But she was real, and he knew it. Their time spent together in the past few weeks had proven her character, and made him feel lacking in comparison. Rose was smart, sweet, hopeful—and yet no one seemed to realize it except for him. To the world, she was simply a maid, which was ridiculous when she was so much more. To him, she was—well, what was she to him? A friend, certainly. A confidante. But that was not enough for Henry any longer.

Not when he could do something about it.

Rose was straightening her apron, adjusting the knot behind her back, when she heard Henry step into the library behind her. She turned to face him, and her cheeks warmed immediately. He looked handsome in his white pressed cravat, his tan jacket finely tailored to suit his arms and shoulders.

"Good morning," she said softly, smoothing the skirts of her plain black dress, the livery all the maids wore. Sometimes she forgot the disparity between them, but today she felt it quite keenly.

"Good morning." His eyes were dancing, bright. "What are we working on today?"

She cleared her throat, looking away. "I am close to finishing the inventory, sir," she said. "Then you shall know precisely where each book is when you finally get around to reading them all."

He laughed, and her stomach gave a curious flip. She liked to make him laugh. No one else found her particularly amusing, but with Henry it was easy. Comfortable, even.

If only she did not have such an *uncomfortable* subject to breach with him. What good could come of it, accusing his own housekeeper of an uncertain crime? Who knew if it even needed reporting? Perhaps she had been discussing grocery deliveries with a footman.

But she knew very well that was not it, and she needed to warn Henry of anything untoward happening amongst his staff.

She stepped forward, clasping her hands before her. "I have something I need to tell you, sir."

But he waved her off. "Whatever it is, it can wait."

"I'm not certain it can—"

He did not seem to be listening. Instead, he crossed the room to her, a mischievous gleam to his eye. "Close your eyes," he commanded.

"What?" She pulled in her chin.

"Close your eyes," he repeated, a little softer, but no less mysteriously. "Please."

She cast him a curious glance before dutifully closing her eyes. His hand took hers, still clasped in front of her, and gently separated them. Her heart quickened and she was suddenly very aware that they stood alone in the library together, with no more than a breath between them. His hands moved lightly on hers, turning it palm upward, his touch sending a shiver across her skin. He dropped something into her palm, small and cool, and then closed her fingers around it.

She knew instantly what it was. Her eyes flew open and she stared at her closed fist for a long moment before releasing her fingers. It was her mother's necklace, the gold rose winking in the morning light.

"How did you know?" she whispered. She looked up at him and found his gaze on her, a more serious expression overtaking the playfulness from before.

"I saw it in the shop window," he said quietly. "If I'd known you were going to sell it that day, I never would have let you."

He was still standing far too close. Rose could hardly breathe with him so near, let alone think. "You hardly knew me then."

"I knew enough," he said. "Though I certainly have not been disappointed in what I've come to know about you since."

She attempted a bit of humor. "My loose tongue hasn't frightened you off?"

His eyes traveled across her face, intent. "Quite the opposite, in fact."

She looked down again at the necklace and tears clouded her eyes as she closed her fingers once more around it, pressing her hand against her chest.

"Thank you, Henry," she breathed.

He dipped his head to catch her eye once again. "You do know that is the first time you have said my name." He looked at her then with such feeling that her chest felt tight, her head light. He moved closer and raised his hand to her face. She hitched a breath, not daring to move as his thumb lightly traced her jawline, his gaze on her continually.

"Rose," he said, voice husky.

Footsteps sounded in the hallway outside the library, quick and decisive. Henry dropped his hand and she nearly leaped away from him, hurrying to the table where she had left her duster. She trembled all over as she scooped it up, turning just as Mrs. Morton appeared in the doorway. She took in the sight of them, alone in the library, and set her jaw, eyes blazing.

"Lord Norcliffe," she said tightly. "Please pardon my interruption, but I have something that I simply must bring to your attention."

Henry did not look at Rose, no doubt an attempt to keep their charade intact. "Yes, what is it?" he said briskly.

Mrs. Morton's face was turning an alarming shade of red. "I regret to inform you that we have a thief in the house."

Rose stared at the housekeeper, still clutching the necklace in her hand. A thief?

Henry shook his head, his eyes narrowed. "I shall require a bit more explanation than that."

"This morning," Mrs. Morton said, her words coming faster now, "I was cleaning the late baroness's room and found her jewelry box stripped of its contents."

Henry froze. "Her jewelry is gone?"

"Yes."

He still did not move, his back stiff. "What of the hand mirror?"

"Gone," Mrs. Morton said. "And when I searched the servants' rooms, determined to find who had committed such a horrible offense, I found this in one of their chambers."

She held up a necklace and Rose nearly had to squint to see it, so blinding was the light that reflected from the diamonds.

"Whose?" Henry demanded, stepping forward. Rose hadn't seen him this angry since that day in the entry. "Whose chamber?"

Mrs. Morton fixed her eyes on Rose, and in a striking moment of clarity, far too late, she realized what was happening.

"Miss Sinclair's," Mrs. Morton said. "I found it in Miss Sinclair's room."

Rose's breaths were coming faster now, panic building inside her. This was it. This was what Mrs. Morton had been planning last night.

"It was all I found," Mrs. Morton continued. "She must have sold the rest of it off."

Rose was hardly paying attention to the housekeeper's words. She was staring at Henry, waiting for a reaction, any reaction. He could not possibly believe she had done this. Could he?

"I've never seen that necklace before," Rose said, her voice weak and shaky. Henry did not turn to look at her, did not even seem to realize she had spoken.

After a few moments, Henry shook his head. "But why would she risk staying here? It does not make any sense."

Rose had never been more grateful for his logical mind. Of course he would not turn on her.

Mrs. Morton shook her head. "She knows I only clean there once a month. I was not due for another fortnight, but decided to clean the linens. Lucky I did, or we'd never have caught her. Miss Sinclair is a thief and a liar, my lord, a minx who has taken this position for one purpose: to steal from you."

Henry stood without moving. Rose's mind was a jumble; what could she say in her defense? That is, if she could convince her tongue to speak. At the moment it was paralyzed by fear and shock.

Finally, he turned to face her. Her heart trembled. There was no kindness in his eyes. His jaw was tight, his shoulders rigid.

"Henry," she whispered. "Please, I promise it was not me. It was Mrs. Morton, I swear. I heard her last night—"

He shook his head and stepped away from her. "You betrayed me, after all I did for you." His voice was hard, furious.

And he left, shouting for Frampton, demanding the butler assign a footman to keep watch over her while another was sent for the constable. Rose gasped for air, her lungs impossibly tight. She stumbled backwards, catching herself on the edge of the table.

The house was in an uproar, but all Rose could see was Mrs. Morton's smirk and the accusing look upon Henry's face, frozen forever in her memory.

Chapter Eleven

It took everything Henry had to look Rose in the eye and renounce her. His stomach turned and his hands were shaking with anger as he spoke, but he did not allow himself to slip. Mrs. Morton had to believe he thought Rose the thief. If she didn't, then the plan he had concocted all of twenty seconds ago would fail before it had even begun.

But the sight of Rose—pale and trembling, her eyes wide in desperation—nearly broke him. Before she could say his name again, plead in that quivering voice of hers, he turned and strode from the room.

A half hour later, he still could not calm himself enough to sit. He'd found himself in his mother's room, not entirely certain how he'd gotten there. He paced, waiting for word from Frampton, his eyes going to the jewelry box on the vanity with every turn of his feet. It was empty, as Mrs. Morton had claimed. When she had first spoken those words, those horrible words accusing Rose, he was ashamed to admit he had given in to a moment of doubt. Was Rose capable of such a thing? She had known about the mirror, after all. He had told her himself. He knew she needed the money. Was she truly that desperate?

But why would she have sold her mother's necklace if she had planned to steal the mirror? It made no sense. And one look at her was all it took to remind him of who she was. She was sweet and kind, endearingly cheerful and unendingly optimistic. His doubts had fled in the space of a breath, and a new realization took hold in his mind. If Rose had not done it, that could only mean that Mrs. Morton *had.* And that was something Henry would not stand for.

When the butler finally slipped soundlessly into his mother's room, Henry looked up at him sharply. "Well?" he demanded.

"All is as you ordered." Frampton came closer, his voice low. "Charlie is watching Mrs. Morton, and the constable should arrive any moment."

"Where is Mrs. Morton now?" He could barely speak her name, so thick was the rage inside him.

"Belowstairs, in the kitchen."

"Good." He moved without hesitation to the door.

"My lord, should you not wait for the constable?"

Henry turned back. "I'll not leave Rose in torment any longer. Send the constable in when he arrives, and inform me if Mrs. Morton comes near the library."

Frampton nodded. "As you wish, my lord."

"You mustn't panic," Rose whispered to herself for the thirtieth time in as many minutes. "You did not do this. Henry will see the truth."

But the lies she told herself were becoming harder to believe. The minutes ticked past and still no one came back into the library to tell her this had all been a terrible mistake. No, this was not a mistake. It was her horrifying reality.

What was the punishment for such a theft? Would she be sent to prison? What would become of Papa when he no longer had anyone to pay for his food and fees?

Rose sank back into her chair, throwing an arm over her mouth to stifle the sobs that forced their way up her throat, her eyes burning with tears.

How could Henry think she had done this? He knew her better than that. Had she not proven herself honest and dependable in all their time together? His trust in the world could not be so broken that he would believe the worst of her this easily. And yet she could not rid herself of his hardened expression, betrayal burning in his eyes.

Amidst her tears, she barely heard the door open across the room. It must be the constable. She scrambled to her feet, swiping away the tears from her cheeks. Should she try and look innocent? But how could she look anything but innocent when that's what she was?

Her thoughts came to staggering halt. It was not the constable stepping into the room, but Henry. He closed the door firmly behind him and turned to her with an unreadable expression. Her heart sank.

She swallowed hard, stepping forward. “Henry, you must know I would never do such a thing. I promise, I have never so much as entered your mother’s room—”

“I know.”

She blinked, her next words catching in her throat. “You—you what?”

“I know, Rose.” He crossed the room before she could take two breaths and stopped before her. “I know you would never betray me like that.”

His grey eyes looked at her with such softness, such tenderness, that she took a step back. “But you said—”

He grimaced. “I am sorry for what I was forced to say. But I had to if I wanted Mrs. Morton to think I did not suspect her.”

She stared at him. Was she imagining this? Were the desperate hopes of her heart influencing her mind? Her hands were shaking uncontrollably. “You do not believe I did it?”

He shook his head, taking her trembling hand and holding it against his chest. “No, I do not. But I do believe you know something about what happened. I need to know everything.”

Rose’s mind was spinning, but relief swelled within her, forcing out the dread that had taken root there. She suddenly felt weak, the whirlwind of the past hour taking its toll on her, and only once Henry had seated her again and repeated the question did she find her voice.

"Last night," she began. "I was outside when I heard Mrs. Morton speaking with a man."

"A man?" he asked sharply. "Did you recognize him? Was he one of the servants?"

She shook her head. "I never saw him, just heard his voice, and I did not know it. He spoke of acting quickly, before it was too late and something was moved. And Mrs. Morton said they needed to avoid suspicion, and that she had a plan in place." She closed her eyes briefly. "It wasn't until Mrs. Morton was accusing me that I realized they were talking about the mirror. I was going to tell you this morning, but she came before I could."

She looked up at him, searching his face for any signs of mistrust. But she saw only determination in his steely eyes.

"What are you going to do?" she whispered.

"Whatever I must," he said. "I will not allow that viperous woman to succeed. I have a footman watching her every move and the constable is on his way. I intend to inform him of everything, and then let him proceed with the investigation as if you truly were guilty."

Her hands went cold and her insides jolted. "What?"

His face softened, his eyes apologetic. "I am sorry, I did not mean to frighten you again. But if we want Mrs. Morton to lead us to both her accomplice and the mirror, she needs to think we have no doubts as to your guilt. I promise I will not allow any harm to come to you."

He took her hand again and pressed it to his lips, and it was difficult to feel anything but the rush of emotion that overwhelmed her senses. His lips were soft on her skin, and she wanted nothing more than to slip into his arms and let the world go on without them. But that was not so easily done as said. He lowered her hand and watched her intently, waiting. She took a steadying breath.

"Tell me what I must do."

Chapter Twelve

The clock ticked softly in the quiet of the library. It was nearing midnight, the flames in the fireplace burning low, but Henry did not feel the least bit tired. Not only had the turmoil of the day rendered sleep entirely impossible, but Rose had finally fallen asleep on his shoulder, exhausted from the trying day. He had no desire to move now, not with her warmth beside him and her soft breaths against his neck.

The constable, Mr. Bowles, sat across the room, arms crossed as he stared into the fire. He looked every bit as alert as Henry felt. It had taken some convincing when they had first told the constable the truth earlier that afternoon. But after he questioned Rose and listened to Henry's words on her behalf, he had been more than willing to join their charade.

Bowles had called Mrs. Morton up for questioning, treating her as if she was a valuable witness and not in fact their only suspect. Henry could not be present for that interview; he was certain he would be unable to sit quietly as Mrs. Morton told her lies. But it had all gone as planned. Mrs. Morton believed that Rose had been arrested, and that there were no suspicions cast upon her at all.

They had been waiting through the long hours of the afternoon and into the evening. Bowles was certain the housekeeper would make her move soon. "Thieves always make mistakes when they think they've escaped," he'd said.

Despite their circumstances, Henry could not find himself disappointed in being forced to spend the entire day in Rose's company. Even when worried, she still managed to smile and laugh with him, and their day passed much quicker than it should have, considering what they were up against. But as darkness settled in, Rose finally gave in to weariness and laid her head against his shoulder. He would have liked to stay this way all night, inhaling her tantalizing scent, feeling her soft hair against his cheek.

But a sharp knock came at the door, and it could only mean one thing.

He nudged Rose, and she sat up immediately, blinking the sleep from her eyes. "It's time," he whispered.

Bowles was already on his feet, moving across the room to the door. Frampton stepped inside and searched the room until he
met Henry's eyes.

"She just slipped out the servants' entrance," he said quietly. "Charlie is certain she is heading to town."

"Let's get on with it," Mr. Bowles growled. "My man at the road will keep an eye on her until we get there."

Henry nodded and was about to stand when he felt Rose's hand slip into his. He turned to her, and his pulse tripped at the concern in her eyes. "Do be careful," she whispered.

Even with her hair a mess and her eyes red from exhaustion and tears, Henry had never imagined anyone so beautiful. He wanted nothing more than to pull her to him and kiss her quite soundly, but now was hardly the time with both Frampton and Bowles watching them.

"I will," he said, and he meant it. He did not know who Mrs. Morton's accomplice was, if he was armed or not, but he had every intention of returning to Rose. In their time together, he'd glimpsed something unfathomable, something he'd never thought to have for himself, and he had no desire to give that up now. "Try to sleep," he said.

She gave him a wry look. "How am I to sleep when my pillow has gone off to catch a thief?"

He gave a soft laugh. "Then I shall return as soon as I can, so I may take up the position again."

She gave his hand one last squeeze, keeping her expression brave. But he saw the fear in her eyes and in her forced smile, and he determined that he would never allow her to be afraid again.

Henry could barely make out the shape of Constable Bowles's shoulders ahead of him in the dark, crouched behind a thick bush outside the Golden Crown, the town's inn. They had met the constable's man and Charlie, the footman, on the outskirts of town, where they both confirmed that Mrs. Morton had entered the inn not five minutes past. Henry and Bowles now waited as the other two men took up positions at the back entrance, prepared to intercept anyone trying to escape.

"Ready?" Bowles asked.

Henry gave a nod. He wanted this over and done with, for Rose's sake.

He followed Bowles as the man rose and strode to the front door. The room was busy, but one glance told him Mrs. Morton was nowhere to be seen. He tightened his hold on his pistol, hidden in the pocket of his great coat. The other guests cast curious looks at him, turning away quickly when he glared at them.

Bowles went to the innkeeper, wiping a table in the corner, and conferred with him. The man's eyes found Henry and stared at him, then gestured to a hall at the back of the room as he spoke.

Bowles returned to his side. "He says Mrs. Morton is in the back parlor. A cloaked man went with her."

"Good," Henry said shortly. "We have them."

"I should ask you to stay out here, my lord." Bowles eyed him. "I do not want to endanger the life of a peer."

"Blast it, man," Henry growled. "It hardly matters who I am."

Bowles gave a swift nod. "If you are sure. I think we ought to approach with discretion. Since they are alone, we might be able to overhear something to aid in our case against them."

At Henry's agreement, they started forward again, this time with slow footsteps and no words between them. They entered the hallway and moved to a closed door at the end, where a faint light flickered from beneath. Bowles motioned for Henry to take the opposite side and they readied their pistols.

Voices spoke from inside, and it took a few seconds for Henry to calm his racing heart enough to hear them.

"You're certain your man is reliable?" came a woman's voice. Mrs. Morton. Henry grit his teeth at the sound. He'd never particularly liked his housekeeper, but neither had he suspected she might steal from him.

She went on. "If I have gone through all this trouble, only to have the man caught as he tries to sell it—"

"He won't be caught."

Henry stiffened at the man's voice, and his head snapped up to stare at Bowles. The constable met his eyes. *Do you know him?* he mouthed.

Henry nodded, barely seeing the man beyond the red haze of anger in his eyes. Oh, he certainly knew that voice.

"You needn't worry over such details, my dear Mrs. Morton. You have played your part well, and now you must trust that I will do the same. This mirror will fetch an impressive price, and the jewels are nothing to scoff at. I assure you that you will have your money."

At that, Bowles gave one sharp nod. Henry took a quick breath, raised his pistol, and threw open the door. Bowles stormed inside, with Henry right after him, heat pulsing through his veins.

Two figures sat before the smoldering fire, a lamp lit beside them. They both leaped to their feet, Mrs. Morton letting out an unladylike screech as she threw herself against the far wall. But Henry was watching the other figure, the familiar silhouette of John Ramsbury, as he lunged toward a small table where a pistol lay.

"Stop!" Bowles shouted. "If you touch that weapon, I will shoot."

Ramsbury stumbled to a halt, staring at them with ragged eyes.

"Step away," the constable demanded, gesturing with a point of his gun. Mrs. Morton stood frozen in the corner, hands clasped to her chest.

Ramsbury did not move. "Henry," he said with a gasping breath. "Thank goodness you're here. I was coming to see you tomorrow, to prove you can trust me. I thought if I could bring you your housekeeper, who plots against you and steals from you, then—"

"Save your lies, John." Henry pointed his pistol directly at his former friend's chest. He would not shoot without provocation, but Ramsbury did not know that, and he rather enjoyed the surge of fear he saw in the man's eyes. "An innocent man does not go for his gun at the sight of the constable."

Footsteps sounded in the hall and the constable's man and Charlie burst into the room. Bowles began directing them, taking Ramsbury's pistol and ordering his arrest. Mrs. Morton wailed from the corner, and Henry watched her with narrowed eyes. All the pieces of the puzzle flew together; Mrs. Morton had worked as housekeeper for the Ramsbury's for years. Their connection was obvious now that he thought to look for it. Even as she was taken sobbing down the hallway, Henry did not feel one ounce of forgiveness towards her; she would have stolen away Rose's future in a heartbeat, and that was something he would never forget.

Ramsbury glared at him as he was also led him from the room, but Henry barely spared him a glance as he sat heavily in one of the empty chairs. For a moment, the old pain returned, the stabbing ache of loss. Ramsbury had taken his parents from Henry with his lies and deceit. Would this wound ever heal entirely?

Bowles approached him then, a leather bag in his hand. "Yours, I believe."

Henry took it and glanced inside. Jewels sparkled at him, the familiar lines of his mother's mirror contrasting against the rough leather. He realized then that throughout the entire day, he had given barely a thought to his mother's missing jewelry or her beloved mirror. His worry had been solely for Rose.

That told him more than anything the truth of what he felt for her. Rose had brought light back into his existence, and if anyone could heal his broken heart, it was she. He did not want to live without her, not when he knew the joy of having her in his life.

Chapter Thirteen

Henry could not sleep that night, his body far too restless after his confrontation with Ramsbury. When he'd returned home, Frampton told him that he had sent Rose to bed as soon as they'd had word that the thieves were caught. Henry had been disappointed, as he'd dearly wanted to see her, but he could not begrudge her the much-needed sleep. He retired to his room, waiting out the dark hours until morning when he could see her again.

As soon as the faintest light of dawn broke against his window, he changed and went downstairs. He was not even certain she would be awake yet, but he could not contain his impatience any longer. Frampton waited for him in the entry.

"Where is she?" Henry asked, not bothering with preamble.

Frampton very nearly smiled, which would have been a sight indeed. Instead, he nodded at the door to Henry's study. "She's waiting to speak with you, my lord."

Henry nodded and started away, but then paused. "Remind me to thank you for everything you did last night, Frampton."

"Of course," he said. "I shall add it to your schedule myself."

Henry smiled as the butler walked away. Even if Mrs. Morton had turned out to be less than loyal, he still counted himself fortunate in his staff.

Especially in his maids.

He strode to his study and stepped inside. Rose was at the window and she turned as he entered. The early morning glow lit her face, the reds and oranges blending with her lovely skin in such a way that caused his heart to pound ferociously in his chest. Her eyes met his and he walked slowly to her, afraid to look away, as if she might vanish into the very air.

"Did you sleep well?" he asked as he came before her. She offered a half smile. "As well as can be expected. I was glad to hear that you apprehended the thieves."

She stood rigidly, her hands tucked behind her, and for the first time Henry realized that there was something not quite right. Her face was not open and free as it should be now that the threat against her was gone. "What is wrong, Rose?" he asked quietly. "What has happened?"

She held up her hand, clasping a letter. "I've another letter from my father's jailer." She swallowed and looked away, but not before Henry saw the tears pooling in her eyes. "Papa is still terribly ill, and the jailer bids me to come immediately or I might not see him alive again."

Henry's chest tightened. He stared at her, his eyes moving over her familiar features, her drooping shoulders, and it took him less than a moment to decide. "Then you do not have any time to waste. You should go to him, immediately."

She shook her head. "I cannot leave now, not when everything is such a mess."

He took her shoulders and willed her to look up at him. Her gaze was erratic, wild almost, and it was all he could do not to pull her against him and hold her safe in his arms. But she did not need that now; she needed his support and help.

"You do not need to worry about me," he said firmly. "The only thoughts in your mind should be for your father. Now hurry, go and pack. You will take my coach and be at Marshalsea by nightfall."

She blinked up at him, her lips trembling. "You are sure?" she whispered.

"I am," he said. "I wish I could accompany you, but I have to manage things here." His insides flared with a new anger at Ramsbury. If that man was not such a scourge on society, Henry would be able to do more to help Rose when she needed him the most. But the house would be in chaos, reeling from the theft, and Bowles had asked him to testify against Ramsbury in the coming days. He could not leave now. He dropped his hands from her shoulders, forcing them to his sides. "Now go pack, and I will order the coach."

She nodded and moved across the room. She stopped with her hand on the doorframe and looked back at him, her eyes watery.

"Thank you, Henry," she whispered, and then she disappeared into the hall.

Before the sound of her steps faded, he had already decided what he would do. She did not need the worries of being away from her position, of hurrying to return as soon as possible. He would release Rose from her debt, do all he could to help her. And she would come back when she could, when her father was well.

Doubt began to wriggle within him. *Would* she return? There were no promises between them. Once she was free of debt, would she find a new life with her father and never look back? He could not have invented all that had grown between them. He loved her, and she must feel something for him. Or was she kind to him simply because she had no choice, because she was in his debt?

He let out a long breath. If she did not come back, then it was her choice, and he would not take that from her.

His wandering eyes paused on his desk, where he'd left his mother's mirror locked in the drawer. An idea sparked. She was leaving, but not before he could make clear how he felt about her. A gesture that she could not possibly misinterpret.

Rose leaned forward in the coach, willing it to move faster. Though they made good time across the countryside south of London, it was still far too slow for the anxiety that gathered inside her, the desperation that reached its cold fingers into her chest. What if she was too late? What if even now her father was taking his last breaths?

She exhaled, trying to break the ceaseless circle of her thoughts. She was already doing everything she could to be at his side.

Though in truth, it was all Henry's doing. If not for his help, she would likely still be waiting for a mail coach, instead of here in this comfortable carriage, with the protection of a coachman and footman.

Henry's face flashed through her mind, from their moment of farewell outside Norcliffe House that morning. He had been somber, his eyes worried as he handed her a satchel. He helped her up into the coach, his steady grip reassuring, and said goodbye in a quiet voice that held a strange note of finality. She hadn't questioned him, her focus completely on reaching her father, but now her thoughts could not help but linger on him.

She glanced at the satchel beside her, still closed. With hours still ahead of her, she gave in to her curiosity and pulled the bag to her. There were several items inside; a letter, bread and cheese, a bag that clinked suspiciously of coins, and a wrapped bundle at the bottom that was particularly hefty. The letter was not sealed, so she opened it.

She read it, and then read it again, staring at the page. It was from Henry, addressed to Papa's jailer, telling him that as the Baron Norcliffe, he forgave Mr. Sinclair's debts against him. The jailer was to send Henry any outstanding fees, and to release Mr. Sinclair to Rose's care immediately.

She lowered the letter, closing her eyes. Oh, Henry. She had never imagined he would do something like this, but now that he had, it seemed like she should have expected it. He stayed behind his towering stone walls, wanting only to keep to himself, but he could not hide his generous heart. Not when she finally knew the man behind the gruff exterior.

She set the letter aside and picked up the bundle from the satchel. It was such an unusual shape, and heavy….

She realized immediately what it was. She held her breath as she pulled away the silk wrappings, uncovering the beautiful hand mirror, all golden engravings and tiny set jewels that shimmered with every movement. She traced her fingers across the frame, her throat tight. Why would he give her this, the thing he valued most in the world?

As she lifted it up, a note fell to her lap.

Rose,

I hope you will accept this gift from me, though I'm certain you will declare it to be far too much. In my estimation, it is still not enough to make up for the life and hope you have brought back to me.

I am determined to ensure you do not have any additional worries as you care for your father, so I release you fully from your debt with no expectation of continued employment. I have included your wages for the past month, as well as extra funds to help with expenses for your father.

Yours,

Henry

Rose stared at the note. What did he mean? Did he not want her to come back? She swallowed, folding the note again, fighting the disappointment that stole inside her. What had she been expecting, a declaration of his feelings and a heartfelt proposal? Henry was a baron; no matter their familiarity during the past weeks, he could never marry someone of her station. Life simply did not happen that way. She should be happy enough for the friendship they'd enjoyed and the new future he had given her.

But her heart would not listen as it ached for all she had left behind in that great, echoing house.

Chapter Fourteen

"Rose?"

Rose had been dipping her cloth in cool water at the wash basin, but spun at the quavering voice. She nearly stumbled crossing the length of their room.

"Papa." She dropped to her knees beside the bed. "You're awake."

His eyes were unfocused, moving erratically around the small room. "Where are we? This is not Marshalsea."

Rose smiled weakly. "No, it is not. We are at an inn."

Her eyes traced over his familiar features—long nose, wrinkled skin, his dark hair beginning to grey—and finally allowed relief to flow inside her. The doctor had not held much hope for his survival, but Rose had not allowed herself to think that way. After three days of fevers and incoherent mumblings, he had finally awoken.

He struggled to sit up in bed and she helped him, propping pillows behind his back. When he was settled once more, he let his eyes rest on her, searching her face.

"How?" was all he managed. "How are you here?"

"Lord Norcliffe," she said softly. "He forgave your debts."

His mouth parted. "The baron? But why?"

His words brought such memories to Rose's mind that she had to look away, not wanting to share the emotions they brought with them. "Did you receive my letter about finding employment with him?"

"Yes." He furrowed his brow. "But you can't have paid it back already."

She took a deep breath. "I hadn't, not yet. This was an act of kindness on his part."

"Kindness?" He could not have sounded more confused. "Lord Norcliffe is not known for his mercy. "I daresay he shall be, after all this."

"I—" His voice cut out and he dropped his eyes, heaving a deep breath. He reached out a shaky hand and took hers. "Oh my child, I wish I could tell you how sorry I am, for betraying your trust, for taking away your future."

Rose shook her head. "Papa, you needn't worry about apologies. You need to rest."

He gave a little cough, waving away her concern. "I cannot rest until I know you forgive me. I have tormented myself these past weeks, believing you might not still love a foolish old man."

Rose closed her eyes and pressed his hand to her lips. "Papa, that is not possible. I shall always love you."

He gave a frail smile. "What did I do to deserve such a daughter?"

"You raised me to be who I am," Rose whispered. "You have made mistakes, but that is not something I would ever allow to come between us."

He rested his head against his pillow. "If only your mother could see the woman you've become."

Rose smiled against the tears and could not find the words to say what she was feeling. She remained silent, grasping his hands firmly.

"How shall we ever repay Lord Norcliffe for his kindness?" he asked. "I still cannot imagine why he would do such a thing."

"There is more to him than you think," she said. "He is not so terrible as everyone claims." She hesitated. "But I have been thinking. I hate to take advantage of his charity, not when having you out of that awful prison is more than enough."

"You're not thinking of returning to work there?" He squinted at her.

"That is precisely what I am thinking," she said. "And you shall not sway me from my course. Once you are well, I am hopeful you might find a position nearby while I return to Norcliffe House to pay our debt—"

"My debt," he murmured, but she ignored him.

"—and once it is paid, we can start again." She exhaled. "It will not be easy, but it is possible."

He squeezed her hand. "I hate to see you turn to service, when I could provide for you."

She shook her head. "I know, Papa, but it is something I must do. Please, let me do it."

He watched her for a long moment, his eyes doubtful as if he knew there was more of her heart involved than she was admitting. But he finally nodded. “Of course. If that is your wish, then who am I to keep you from it?”

Henry did not think of himself as the brooding type. He could be cross, yes, rude even, but he did not generally take to moping. He considered it to be a waste of time.

But he had no other way to describe his mood since Rose had left a fortnight before. How had one woman come to rule over his emotions so entirely in such a short amount of time? And now she was gone, with no reason to return.

Perhaps she might come back for you, a small voice whispered in his mind as he sat at his desk. But why would she, with her father’s debt forgiven? After all, he had never offered for her, nor could he have while her father’s life was in danger. He’d had word from Marshalsea that Mr. Sinclair was recovering well at a nearby inn, but had yet to hear from Rose herself.

The door opened and Frampton stepped inside, wearing perhaps the oddest look he’d ever seen on the man’s face before. His eyes were alive, his lips twitching with a barely concealed smile.

"What is it, Frampton?" Henry spoke a bit shortly, irritated to have been interrupted amidst his brooding.

"You have a visitor, my lord." Frampton's voice fairly danced with delight.

Henry grunted. "You know I do not accept visitors."

"I took it upon myself to allow this one," he said.

Henry narrowed his gaze, but before he could argue, Frampton had disappeared with a bow, leaving the door open. Then a figure, a lovely and familiar figure, stepped into the doorway.

Henry gaped at Rose as he sat frozen, hand gripping his pen. *She had come back*. He drank in the sight of her: dark hair peeking from beneath her bonnet, her brown eyes watching with trepidation as she moved further into the room and dropped into a curtsy.

"R-rose," he stammered, then cleared his throat before attempting again. He was a baron, for heaven's sake, and he ought to sound like one. He set down his pen and stood from his desk. "I did not know you had returned."

"Yes, sir," she said with a hesitant smile. "Papa is recovering well and looking for a position."

"I'm glad." His words sounded terribly forced, but there was nothing for it. "And you are well?"

"I am." Her smile faded, and her expression turned serious. "I wish to thank you for the mirror. I will treasure it always."

He nodded, unable to think of anything to say. *She had come back.*

She went on. "And I wish to express my gratitude for your generosity to my father. I hope you know I never expected it of you, considering our friendship—"

"No, I—" He tried to speak, but she pressed on.

"—and I wanted you to know that even though you have forgiven his debts, I am still determined to work until they are paid in full. If the maid's position has not yet been filled, I am more than willing—"

"You cannot be serious," he interrupted, staring at her.

She blinked. "Oh. I see. There is no position anymore. Well, then I shall find work in town, and make monthly payments—"

"Rose," he said firmly. "Please, stop."

She pressed her lips together, clearly not pleased at having to cease her talking. He walked toward her slowly, studying her intently. She truly thought to simply take up her old post, work in his house again as a maid?

He shook his head as he came to a stop before her. "Rose, you are the single most stubborn and captivating woman I have ever met, but if you think I will allow you to work one more minute in my house, you must also be mad."

Her eyes widened. "But I—"

He placed a finger on her lips. "I am in earnest, Rose. Let me speak."

He brushed the backs of his fingers along her cheek, as he'd imagined doing dozens of times during their mornings together. She shivered under his touch.

"Rose," he said quietly. "For the past two years, I have been trapped in a shadow of anger and regret. I thought I wanted a life of quiet solitude. But you've shown me that I can have so much more than I ever imagined. I can have peace and laughter. Even love."

She was staring at him, but he did not hesitate. He moved closer, taking both her hands and raising them. "So I must ask you, Rose Sinclair, if you will share my life with me. Because there is nothing I want more than you as my wife."

Her mouth parted, and then she closed it again, pressing her lips together. Her eyes filled with tears. "Henry," she whispered. "Do you mean it?"

He could stop himself no longer. He pulled her to him and his lips found hers, soft and sweet. He kissed her gently at first; she seemed so fragile in his arms, so breakable. But then her hands discovered his cravat and she tugged him closer, igniting a fire deep within him. She kissed him back, with all the vitality he'd come to expect from her. He pressed his hands against her back, her warmth and scent intoxicating, and she leaned into him, her small frame molding perfectly against him.

When at last they broke apart, she stared up at him with such tenderness that his heart stumbled. He'd never imagined someone might look at him that way, let alone someone he loved with all that he was.

"Is that a yes?" He pressed his forehead against hers.

"It is," she said with a smile, her voice a bit breathless. "On one condition."

He pulled away slightly to see her clearer. "And what would that be?"

Her eyes lit with mischief. "You must promise to read *Robinson Crusoe*."

He gave a laugh, throwing back his head. "That, my dear," he said, still chuckling, "is an arrangement I am all too willing to make."

Then he kissed her again, his hands cradling her face. Henry finally realized what emotion had reflected in her eyes, because he felt the same one burning in his chest.

Happiness.

And now that he had it, he would never, ever let it go.

Author's Note

I hope you enjoyed this novella! If so, please consider leaving a review or telling your friends. Authors very much depend on readers like you to help build our audiences, and every little bit helps!

I would love to connect with you on social media! Come find me on Facebook and Instagram for more info about me, my books, and the writing life. To find updates on upcoming books or to sign up for my newsletter, stop by my website at www.authorjoannabarker.com.

Thank you!

Titles by Joanna Barker

The Truth about Miss Ashbourne
Beauty and the Baron
Miss Adeline's Match (Coming April 2019)

Joanna Barker was born and raised in northern California. She discovered her love for historical fiction after visiting England as an eleven-year-old, and subsequently read every Jane Austen book she could get her hands on. After graduating Brigham Young University with a degree in English, she worked as an acquisitions editor before devoting herself full-time to writing. She enjoys music, chocolate, and reading everything from romance to science fiction. She lives in Utah and is just a little crazy about her husband and two wild-but-loveable boys.

All of Joanna's published works are available on Amazon.com.

Made in United States
Orlando, FL
06 December 2021